LOVE
ON 3
wheels

Anurag Anand

Srishti
PUBLISHERS & DISTRIBUTORS

SRISHTI PUBLISHERS & DISTRIBUTORS
Registered Office: N-16, C.R. Park
New Delhi – 110 019
Corporate Office: 212A, Peacock Lane
Shahpur Jat, New Delhi – 110 049
editorial@srishtipublishers.com

First published by
Srishti Publishers & Distributors in 2015

10 9 8 7 6 5 4 3 2 1

Cover art and design – Shilpa Shanker Narain (behance.net/shilpas)

Burn me down to ashes,
Lend me to the flames.
Rise again I valiantly shall,
For Love is but my name.

28th December

Hope and optimism so often become our deliverances from the drudgery of routine, and these qualities Sargam possessed in abundance. Someone had once told her that the start to a day holds the key to how rest of it would unfold, and since then, she had made it a point to wake up with a smile and thank the gods for the good that beckoned her.

The Gods mostly ignored her advance expression of gratitude, but Sargam seldom noticed. She was convinced that her present was merely a hiatus before destiny propelled her to the heights she was meant to scale.

Today morning had been no different. She had left her bed enthusiastically, sensing some concealed promise even in the chilly dawn, before heading to the kitchen for preparing the only indulgence she permitted herself – her early morning cup of tea.

Holding the steaming cup between her palms, she perched on the cane chair next to her bedroom window and peered out. The city, at least most of it, was yet to emerge from its slumber. She watched the fog struggling against the breeze to claim its sovereignty as she layered her worries of the past few weeks with a liberal surge of autogenous sanguinity and cheerfulness. She sat there for nearly fifteen minutes, burying her apprehensions and prepping herself for yet another beginning.

At 8.30, Sargam emerged from the dilapidated complex where she lived in a smallish two-room flat with her parents. Both, her mother and her father were still asleep and she left the house without bothering to disturb them. This didn't trouble her any more. Initially, yes, but she had come to terms with their apathy in due course, even before she had started working.

As she emerged on the main road, she caught sight of Sharib. He was wiping the already sparkling windshield of his auto rickshaw across the road. Thank God he's here, she told herself as she made for the auto and slid inside wordlessly. Sharib too returned to his seat and jerked the handlebar to bring the vehicle to life.

'Office madam?' he enquired, to which she nodded her head, catching his eye in the rearview mirror.

It had been over a year that she had been travelling to office and back in the same auto. Even though she couldn't recall a single instance when the auto-wallah had stood her up, she couldn't avoid the pang of inexplicable anxiety she felt each time she stepped out of her house or the office. What if he wasn't there? What if he'd found a more profitable passenger to ferry?

Sargam had a latent fear, a phobia of sorts, of the Delhi auto rickshaws and their drivers. Perhaps it was the scuffle she had witnessed as a child when the drivers from a nearby auto stand had beaten her father black and blue over a petty row. The scuffle was over something paltry – where he had parked his scooter, as far as she could recall – and she had watched in horror, howling her guts out, as they had mercilessly kicked and slapped him. Or maybe it was just a perception she had formed because of the accounts she had heard of their disorderly and brash conduct. The fact nevertheless was that Sargam considered autos as a social malady and had avoided them for as long as she could help.

The Delhi Metro and DTC (Delhi Transport Corporation) buses had served her well till her college years, but the equation changed as soon as she joined her job. She was working as a Secretary, at least as per the proclamation on her appointment letter, with a small trading company which had its offices in Okhla Industrial Area. Including the proprietor, Mr. Ahuja, there were a total of six pairs of hands in the office, and as a result any of them could find themselves doing the other's job at the boss's whim. There were times when even the office boy would be ordered to key-in data in an Excel sheet, a task he would gladly take up for the supposed importance it accorded him.

Mr. Ahuja was a kind man in his own peculiar way. He was extremely empathetic and understanding as long as it didn't call for a penny or two to leave the safety of his pockets. When it came to business, or anything else that could have possible monetary ramifications, he was uncompromising and ruthless. He ensured that he got his money's worth out of each one of his employees, including Sargam. An obvious offshoot of this was his near obsession with adherence to office timings. On her very first day he had made it amply clear to Sargam that she needed to be in office by nine every morning. And since then the message had been reinforced more than once when she had witnessed her colleagues being reprimanded for breaching the sacred high-water mark.

The compulsion of reaching office on time coupled with the lack of metro connectivity between Srinivaspuri and Okhla forced Sargam to surrender herself to the mercy of Delhi's auto-wallahs. In the initial weeks, she tried hailing random autos by flagging them off the main road, but quickly the futility of it all became apparent. Not only did she have to leave the house well in advance, praying that she found a willing one in time, but given her dependency, she also found herself paying more than the usual fare on a regular basis.

She tried engaging autos to ferry her on a daily basis, most of whom turned her down. Of the three who agreed, one never showed up, one turned out to be as dependable as a rolling dice and the third gave up after rendering two weeks of service. Mornings were fine, he said, but it was a challenge for him to make it to Okhla from wherever he was for the evening pickup. 'I have to refuse passengers and come empty all the way,' he explained. Sargam even offered to increase their pre-negotiated price, but he was beyond convincing.

Then, when she was once again down to hailing autos arbitrarily, she met Sharib. He was parked outside her apartment complex the first day that she engaged him. It was a usual uneventful ride – impersonal and detached, an auto-wallah ferrying a nameless passenger to her desired destination. And so, when Sargam found him at the same spot the next morning, she failed to even recognize him.

'Madam, do you go to office at the same time every day?' The driver was the one to initiate conversation. It was a lame sounding question, but Sargam was quick to latch on to the opportunity it had unwittingly created for her. Sharib, unlike her past experiences with his professional comrades, did not negotiate on the price and readily agreed to the proposed arrangement. He even shared his mobile number with her in case she was unable to spot him someday.

'They say the temperature might fall further over the coming days,' Sharib shouted over the noise of the sputtering auto. Over the past fourteen odd months, their familiarity had reached a point where he would make an odd remark or two and she would add her two bits to it. She had opened her mouth to voice an agreement when the ring of her mobile phone interrupted her. The caller was Geeta, one of the few friends from college who had stuck on with Sargam.

'Hey, how are you?' Sargam greeted her cheerfully. By now Sargam had mastered the art of holding a telephonic conversation while travelling in an auto. The Boss didn't take kindly to personal calls being entertained at work, and at home there were her nosey parents to watch out for. These auto rides were the only time she got for connecting with her social circle, howsoever minuscule it happened to be.

She had cupped her left hand over the mouthpiece and was speaking in a pitch that made her words travel right into Sharib's ears. Whether he wished to or not, he couldn't help overhearing her side of the dialogue.

'I am okay... am on my way to work now... I was waiting for your call yesterday.' Pause.

'No no... that's fine... Ya, I did meet him. Mummy wouldn't have it any other way. But it was just the same. He is a creep with a single-track mind.' Pause.

'The same old spiel about what all I am missing out on and how he can wave a magic wand and set things right for me. You need to hear him to believe the things he can say.' Pause.

'Yeah, right! Why don't you go ahead instead? I can help with the introductions if you want.' A tinge of sarcasm followed by laughter! Pause.

'You can be such a bitch when you want to...' Feigned annoyance followed by more laughter!

'Yeah, he did make that offer again... What do you think? Of course I declined. Okay, I need to go now... have reached office...

Why don't you drop by tomorrow, it's Sunday and there is plenty we need to catch up on… Sure. Bye.'

She glanced at her wrist watch as she stepped into the office. It was 8.55 a.m. She had made it in time yet again. She would live to see another day.

◆

The day was sliding past, once again failing on the promise of possibilities that Sargam had envisaged of it. She had spent most of her day tracking an overdue shipment and preparing invoices, tasks that were as mundane as rolling chapatis is to a housewife. The clock on her desktop monitor was slowly ticking towards five, half an hour before she could leave office, when the intercom came alive with a shrill. The Boss's name was flashing on the display screen.

Tentatively she reached for the receiver. She knew from experience that Mr. Ahuja's summon just before pack-up time could translate into several hours of uncompensated overtime.

'Sargam, can you step in for a minute?' the Boss said. The 'a minute' was a euphemism that Mr. Ahuja was known to use liberally for disarming his employees. His minutes could sometimes prove longer than those of a dysfunctional clock.

'Yes sir,' she said, stepping into the only enclosed cabin that the 600 square feet office could boast of.

'Come. Sit down,' he replied, sifting through a bunch of papers to pick up a brown envelope. Holding the envelope in one hand, he continued, 'You have met Ramamurthy, haven't you?'

Sargam had met Ramamurthy on a couple of occasions in the past. He was the manager of a garment export firm down south, whose consignments were shipped to buyers by Sargam's employer.

Although Ramamurthy's firm was one of their regular customers, the quantum of their business wasn't enough for them to qualify as one of Mr. Ahuja's premier customers.

She nodded her affirmation.

'He is in Delhi today. I hear he's been speaking to some of our competitors and seeking quotes from them for his business. I was to meet him today evening, but something urgent has come up at home because of which I won't be able to make it,' he began. His appraising eyes were affixed on Sargam as he described the task he expected her to take on.

'I would have sent Partha to see him, but Ramamurthy has never met him. Other than me, you are the only one he knows and will be comfortable discussing business with. I was scheduled to meet him in the lobby of The Park. I suggest that you go there, carry a bouquet or something with you, and convey my apologies for not being able to make it. Tell him that his business is important to us; treat him to a cup of coffee if you have to, and just when you are leaving, give him this packet with my best compliments. That should take care of him,' he said, flashing a rare smile. Sargam sensed a hint of conspiracy in Mr. Ahuja's sneer, and for a moment she even considered voicing one of the many questions that had begun to sprout within her head. But the thought passed in the same flash that it had occurred, leaving her to meekly accept the envelope from her boss.

She returned to her seat and consigned the packet to her purse, cursing slightly under her breath. Not only was her evening ruined, but she even ran the risk of being summoned to office the next day, a Sunday, to brief Mr. Ahuja about the meeting. There was just that slight chance that he would be satisfied with merely a telephonic update, a prerequisite for which was the meeting's outcome to be in line with his expectations. And to think of it, she'd been planning to spend the day gossiping with Geeta and making her long-due trip to the parlour.

At 5.30 sharp she got out of the office and made for the usual spot where her auto-wallah would be waiting. 'I need to go to the Park hotel today,' she instructed. 'And if there is a florist somewhere along the way, I need a couple of minutes there as well.'

Sharib assimilated the instructions with a nod and set the vehicle in motion. His destination was The Park hotel in Nehru Place.

Sargam would never admit, but a sense of nervous anticipation was brewing within her regarding the impending meeting. She was not alien to such client engagements, only this was the first time she was heading out for one on her own. Who knows, she thought, this might be my big chance. If I pull this one off, Mr. Ahuja might consider me for more such solo assignments. A raise or perhaps a promotion too might be in the offering.

Her reverie was broken by Sharib. 'Madam, should I stop here?'

The auto was already in the left lane and had slowed down considerably. Just ahead of them, on the roadside, was a florist's stall.

'Yes please,' she said, unzipping her purse to pull out the wallet.

The vehicle stopped meters ahead of the florist, perilously close to the pavement. Sargam turned towards Sharib, intent on asking him to pull the auto ahead so that she could get out comfortably. But he was already engaged in a conversation. A bike carrying two helmet-clad youths had pulled up beside the auto, and Sharib, craning his neck and gesticulating with his hand, was assisting them with directions to someplace.

'Bhaiya, I will be back in a minute,' she said, smiling to herself for having borrowed her boss's catch phrase. Squeezing herself out of the auto, she jumped onto the pavement and stepped towards the flower stall.

She picked up a bouquet of pink carnations and white roses, bundled around a bunch of iris stems.

'Seven hundred rupees,' the vendor quoted.

'That's too much,' she said. 'I will take it for five hundred rupees. Not a paisa more.' The cost of the bouquet was to be billed to the company, but even then Sargam couldn't get herself to splurge heedlessly. The florist mumbled something to the effect of flowers becoming expensive in the winter season even as he reached out for the bouquet to give it a final touch-up.

Armed with the bouquet, Sargam resumed her journey. The hotel was not far from where she was, but the peak-hour traffic made a struggle of each yard they had to scale. It was twenty minutes later that the auto stopped in front of the hotel entrance.

'Take it inside,' she instructed Sharib, hoping to avoid walking with her heels on the cobbled path streaming from the gate towards the portico.

'Autos are not allowed inside, madam,' Sharib returned apologetically.

'Oh. Okay! How much?'

'If you won't be long, I could wait here for you,' Sharib offered.

'No, that's fine. I might take some time here, so you carry on,' she said, handing him exact change for their pre-negotiated daily fare. Although the distance she had travelled today was lesser than usual, she was in no mood for petty haggling. Moreover, these little concessions, she knew, were an investment towards the larger convenience that Sharib brought about in her life.

As she stepped inside the hotel lobby, Sargam found the grandeur and opulence just a wee bit unnerving. Exceptionally high chandelier-clad ceilings, tawny light bathing the plush upholstery and the sweet mix of natural and synthetic fragrances, this was a world she was yet to get accustomed to.

She peered around, hoping to spot the familiar face of Ramamurthy, but in vain. Probably he hadn't arrived as yet. She was contemplating calling him when her mobile phone rang. It was Mr. Ahuja.

'Have you reached the hotel?'

She told him she had.

'Ramamurthy just called. He is caught up in traffic somewhere and will take another twenty minutes to reach. I thought I would let you know,' he apprised her.

Cursing under her breath, Sargam approached the empty sofa ahead of her and parked herself on it. For a few minutes she kept fiddling with her phone and then, on an impulse, she unzipped her purse. She was meaning to take out the packet her boss had given her for Ramamurthy. But the packet was not there.

She rummaged through the purse to look for it, digging through her hair-brush, nail paints, lipsticks and several forms of junk that had accumulated ever since she had last cleaned it. But the packet was nowhere to be found.

She shut her eyes trying to remember if she had forgotten the packet back in the office. No, she hadn't. She clearly recalled having deposited it in her purse. Where could it have vanished then?

As the realization that she had lost the packet dawned upon her, she felt a rapid gush of wind blow between her ears. Her head, it seemed, had turned hollow and the only sensation she was left with was the whooshing noise of the breeze within. She had an inkling of what the package contained and the thought of having lost it was petrifying.

With trembling hands she picked up her phone and dialled Mr. Ahuja's number. After the second ring, she heard his gruff voice on the line.

'Sir... Sir...,' she tried talking, but her vocabulary seemed to have dried out.

'What?'

'Sir, the packet you had given me… The one I had to give to Ramamurthy, I can't find it,' she somehow spoke.

'WHAT?' Ahuja screamed. 'What do you mean you can't find it?' His sounded as though Sargam had just informed him that his wife had eloped with her driver.

'I mean… I had kept it in my purse, and now it's not there,' she mumbled.

'How can it not be there? It doesn't have legs to walk away on its own, does it? Unless somebody has helped it disappear, it has to be where you kept it,' he continued. Unable to think of a response, Sargam chose to remain quiet.

'You know what was there in the packet, don't you?'

'Err… No sir. I hadn't opened it,' she slurred.

'Okay, if you say so, I believe you,' he retorted with words dripping in sarcasm. 'In that case, allow me to educate you about the contents of the packet. It contained money, one lakh rupees to be precise. I don't care where the packet has vanished, but I need every one of the hundred thousand rupees back. Do you hear me?'

Ahuja continued speaking, but Sargam was no longer listening. One lakh rupees! She had never even set eyes on that kind of money, knowingly at least. Her boss would skin anyone alive for a tenth of that amount. The blunder was obviously going to leave her unemployed, but her immediate concerns were about the whereabouts of the money. Where had it disappeared from her bag? How was she going to make good the loss?

'I thought you were a nice girl, simple and dependable, but I should have known better than to trust you,' Mr. Ahuja's monologue was dripping in her ears like drops of acid.

It was evident that she had been sent there to bribe Ramamurthy. But, with the money out of the equation, was there any point in going ahead with the meeting? She was trying to get a grip on her thoughts, but it was proving exceedingly difficult in wake of her boss's constant babbling.

'Don't think you are going to get away with it. I will have you and your whole family rotting behind bars till I get my money back,' he was persistent. She was thinking of a plausible excuse to disconnect the call when the excuse materialized in person. She caught Ramamurthy making his way across the lobby towards her.

'Ramamurthy is here, I will have to call you back,' she hurriedly uttered before disconnecting the call and muting the volume of her ringer. Ahuja could always call on Ramamurthy's number and ask for her, but she was hoping that he would want to avoid dragging a customer into a matter such as this.

'Hello Ms. Jaw-shee,' Ramamurthy greeted her with his usual effervescence, pronouncing 'Joshi' in a manner that only he could. 'What's the matter? You look as if you have just seen a ghost... or did I scare you? Now, Rama isn't all that scary... is he?' he said, flashing his spotless dentures.

'Hello Mr. Murthy,' she replied, feigning a smile. 'You are right, I am indeed in a fix and you are the only person who can help me out.'

Sargam began narrating her story to a completely baffled Ramamurthy. She hadn't planned this. It was merely an instinct she had decided to pursue, and that gave her account the honesty and sincerity it needed.

She told him about the packet that she was meant to deliver to him and how she had lost it. She went on to confide in him of her conversation with Mr. Ahuja and his accusation that it was she who had misappropriated the money.

'You know me, Mr. Murthy. I would never do such a thing,' she continued, tears brimming her eyes. 'All I ask of you is one day. By Monday morning, I will get you the money. Somehow. Anyhow. Please trust me just this once and I will not disappoint you… Please.'

Sargam had no idea where the money had gone or how she was going to replenish it, but her words seemed to have acquired a mind of their own. They were dropping from her lips unassisted.

Ramamurthy took a few seconds to assimilate the information before speaking. 'Had you been making this request on behalf of your employer, I probably wouldn't have given it a second thought. But, as I understand, the matter is slightly different now,' he began thoughtfully.

'Fine, I am in Delhi for another couple of days, so you can give me the money by Monday morning, but no later than that please. Rama understands your problem, you understand his… okay? The money needs to go to my seniors and they won't wait for very long. If they don't get it by Monday, rest assured, Ahuja can forget about doing any business with us.'

She had got herself a momentary reprieve, but it was momentary at best. She now needed to figure out a way to get the money back from wherever it had disappeared. As she stepped out of the hotel, Sargam pulled out her phone and sent a text message to her boss.

'Met Rama. Have told him that I will arrange the money by Monday morning. He is fine with it. Will keep you posted,' she wrote. The last thing she wanted was to engage in another dialogue with Ahuja. There was much on her mind and she had little time to sort it all out and emerge unscathed from the situation.

Sargam Joshi

Sargam was technically from the hills up north. 'Technically,' because her father, Lalkrishna Joshi had migrated to Delhi from a village in Pithoragarh district, now a part of the state of Uttrakhand. But that was nearly two-and-a-half decades back. Three years before Sargam was even born.

Although her blunt features and naturally radiant skin betrayed her ancestry, that was about all there was of her link to the hills.

Lalkrishna had moved to Delhi the same year that his own mother had died. His father had already succumbed to a severe bout of tuberculosis in the preceding year, and being the only child he was left with no immediate family to bind him to his roots.

Of course, there were those friends and relatives who would visit him every once in a while, but that was typically to seek shelter while travelling to the city on some or the other unconnected business. And with time even those visits tapered away, sequestering the family of four in their chosen habitat.

Lalit, Sargam's elder brother was six months old when Lalkrishna had got his appointment letter from the Public

Works Department (PWD), Delhi. He was to join the Executive Engineer's office as a junior clerk. Disregarding the mild hesitation his wife had dared to voice, he had taken up the offer and moved to Delhi. It had taken the family some time to adjust to the ways of the big city, but they had eventually become one with its pulsating rhythm. It was with Sargam's arrival that the monotony of their lives was once again disturbed.

The earliest childhood memories Sargam had were of playing with her elder brother, running away with his books or his wooden bat and deriving perverse pleasure out of the resulting frustrations. But when it came to her, Lalit was hardly able to persist with his annoyance. Within minutes of every conflict, most of which were deliberately effected by little Sargam, the brother-sister duo would be found sharing a hearty laugh or cuddling up to each other.

Once Sargam started attending school, the same one that Lalit went to, her elder brother cum friend readily took on the role of her protector and guide. She felt a sense of comfort and security with Lalit being around, be it in the school bus or within the premises of the institution.

All other memories from her childhood were pretty obscure and hazy; of her mother, mellow and dutiful, expending her hours within the confines of the kitchen; of her father, authoritarian and remote, buried within the folds of a newspaper or glued to the television set.

When Sargam's friends at school would tell her about their own parents, the equations they shared and the things they indulged in together – trips to the amusement park and movie theatres, vacation jaunts to visit their relatives – she would find the narratives as unreal as the fairytales from her favourite bedtime book. It was simply unthinkable for her to be accompanied by her parents in anything that spelt fun or leisure.

Of course her parents never shirked away from providing for her. Her school fees, clothes, stationery, food, would all be made available, like for Lalit, but that is where the buck stopped. There were no unwanted conversations, no undue expressions of love and virtually no participation of their parents in their lives. It was an extremely formal relationship, perhaps some tenets from the hills that their parents were clinging on to and which the families of their friends had never known.

The passing years worked towards ironing out the infantile creases in the relationship that Sargam shared with her brother. The youthful jollity of their interactions was overcome by dictates of convention and suddenly her life had acquired aspects that she was unable to disclose or discuss with Lalit.

The signs were there, she was growing up into an attractive young lady and the boys in school, and later college, would validate this through their admiring gaze, nervous attempts to strike conversation and enduring efforts to gain her favour. Sargam's upbringing did not allow her to encourage them like some girls in her acquaintance did. But there was nothing to stop her from privately savouring the attention that came her way. And this, among others, was one facet of life she preferred to keep concealed from Lalit. Her brother, she knew, was as possessive about her as she was about him and who knew how he would react to other boys making advances at her.

She still remembered the day she had missed her bus back from college. She had been standing at the bus stand, fighting her fears and priming herself to hail an auto rickshaw when Varun, one of her overt admirers, had offered to drop her home on his motorbike. It had seemed lesser of the two evils and, albeit reluctantly, she had accepted the offer.

Barring a few casually exchanged words, mostly muffled by the gushing wind, the ride proved uneventful. The two-wheeler was clearly more efficient than her usual ride and soon Varun was swerving it inside the gates of her apartment complex. As luck would have it, at precisely that moment, Lalit was heading out of the house. He saw Sargam getting off the bike. Their eyes met for a split-second and what she saw in them sent a shiver running down her spine. She couldn't immediately decipher the look in her brother's eyes or the resulting stab of fear she had experienced momentarily. So, bidding Varun goodbye, she ambled home.

Her father was perched on the wood-framed sofa watching television and the cling-clang from the kitchen betrayed her mother's whereabouts. Nothing unusual, she noted, before heading to the room she shared with her mother. The air within the house was typical too, as it had been for the past eight months, tense and weighty, but Sargam could feel a strange new lump in her throat.

'What the heck! I haven't done anything wrong. Why should I be harbouring any guilt about having taken a lift from a classmate?' she told herself. But the obstinate lump persisted.

Lalit returned home in the evening. A part of Sargam had been hoping that she had read too much into the incident and that Lalit would be normal upon his return. But that was not to be. He appeared to be avoiding her. Even during dinner time hardly a word was exchanged between the two, unnoticed by their parents of course. The pervading gloom had acquired unbearable proportions, and Sargam, unable to swallow any more of the food, abruptly got up and receded to her room.

Her brother had finished college just as she was preparing to step into one, about eight months back. The day his graduation results were declared, he had come home with a bar of her favourite chocolate. He was elated at having passed in first division and

Sargam was the only one he could think of sharing his joy with. However, it turned out to be one of those rare occasions when even an otherwise unresponsive Lalkrishna decided to voice his pride and happiness over his son's success. It was a special day indeed, but the shower of joy it brought with it proved transitory at best.

It started with harmless suggestions and counsel that Lalkrishna began doling out to his son. He had developed a sudden and mysterious interest in Lalit's career, more specifically his entry into the job market. And this, Sargam could see, wasn't going particularly well with Lalit.

As of his own, Lalkrishna was still working with PWD, as a Senior Clerk now. With only a couple of years to go for his retirement, he went to office once or twice every week and that too barely for a few hours. His remaining hours were spent in front of the TV on his favoured wooden sofa. That, and ordering his wife around, Lalkrishna seemed to have no other pursuable interests in life. He appeared content in his unenterprising and unsocial existence and this sometimes irked Sargam beyond measure.

Watching her father idling away his life, she would often swear to herself about making something more worthwhile out of her own. She would wince each time she saw him sprawled aimlessly on the sofa. And then, to soothe her nerves, she would tell herself about the fictional fortunes that life had in store for her – concealed and protected, to be revealed only when the time was ripe. It was perhaps this escape that had embedded itself deep in her psyche to turn her into an eternal optimist.

Thus, when Lalit began reacting to Lalkrishna's interference, evasively to begin with and confrontationally later, she was able to see reason in his defiance. A man who had done nothing with his life but to make his wife cook food of his choosing had no right to dictate terms. Lalit was mature enough to make his own decisions.

With time, as Lalit's jobless status persisted, Lalkrishna's comments began to sound more like poking taunts and Lalit's retorts began to border around rebelliousness. The tension within the household continued to mount, and Sargam, in her helplessness, could only commiserate with her brother's misery. His frustrations were so evident that at times she couldn't help but wonder if employment had actually been eluding him all this while or had he begun to skirt opportunities as an extreme measure of his defiance.

A showdown was inevitable and one evening it did play out. Sargam was in her room when the screams and yells emerged from the living area. The immediate cause of the confrontation remained unknown to her, but she appeared on the scene just in time to catch her father and brother shouting at each other like blood-thirsty hounds. She stood gaping, her legs trembling with an unknown fear, as she witnessed the blatant disregard for kinship and blood-ties within the walls of her own home.

Her mother's intervention prevented the matter from escalating any further than it already had and the subject was not raised within the household ever again. It was as if the ugly spat had never taken place – an unspoken escape from the shame it brought to the warring factions as well as the two onlookers. Lalkrishna stopped meddling in Lalit's affairs from that day. In fact, all ties of communication between the two were severed post the incident.

Lalit and Lalkrishna were still not on talking terms and their nonverbal disapproval of the other's existence was the prime cause of the continuing strain. And to add to the afflictions, she too seemed to have lost Lalit's favour now.

Deciding to end the matter once and for all, she arose from the bed. The luminous hands of the wall clock were closing in on midnight. Sometime while she was lost in her reverie, her mother had come into the room and slid beside her. A soft hum confirmed that she was sound asleep already.

Sargam tiptoed out of the room and, guided by the dim light seeping in through the window, made for the mattress spread against one of the drawing room walls. The mattress was Lalit's makeshift bed. He had been sleeping there since his showdown with Lalkrishna.

She had to bend down and look real closely at Lalit's face to figure if he was still awake. Awake he was and the whites of his eyes were staring right back at her.

'What happened? What's wrong with you?' she whispered.

Lalit propped himself on the mattress and turned to face her. After a moment's silence he said, 'You damn well know what's wrong! Don't you?'

'I don't know. You tell me. Are you behaving like this because Varun dropped me home?'

'Yeah, I am the one behaving strangely. But isn't that a usual fare in this house?' he returned scornfully. 'And you don't think there is anything wrong in riding behind strangers on their motorbikes?'

'Bhaiya, you are exaggerating now. Varun is no stranger. He is a classmate of mine. And it's not as if I ride with him every day. I had missed my bus and so when he offered to give me a ride, I accepted it. That's all that is there to it,' she explained.

To begin with, Lalit wasn't particularly receptive to Sargam's arguments.

'You don't know these Delhi guys. I move around with them all the time. I know exactly how they think and what they talk. For you it might be just a lift, but how do you know what's playing on his mind?' he reasoned.

However, Sargam's reason and logic eventually got the better of him and he was forced to concede. 'Okay, I might be overreacting, but that's for a reason. I can't bear anyone taking advantage of my little sister. You are too naïve. If anyone ever hurts you, I will kill the bastard,' he said in a voice creaking with emotions.

It was touching, his concern and love for her. Sargam could feel a few drops trickling down her cheeks involuntarily. On an impulse, she reached out and embraced his sprawled form.

'I love you bhaiya,' she said as he returned the embrace. There were tears in his eyes too.

Sargam was relieved, but Lalit's arguments had strengthened her conviction that she could no longer go about spilling all her beans to him. They had both grown up and somewhere along the way their views on certain aspects of life had taken divergent turns. She had no way of knowing then that her fears were unfounded. Lalit wasn't going to remain within meddling distance of her life for long.

A few months later, Lalit confided in her about having found a job in France. A friend of his had gone there through an agent and was doing reasonably well for himself. It was at this friend's beckoning that Lalit had conducted a thorough research about the opportunity and was now ready to take the plunge.

'France, but why so far? Can't you find a job here in Delhi itself? How will you stay there? And what is the kind of work you will be doing there?' Sargam had bombarded him with a barrage of questions.

'How does it matter what the work is? It isn't as if I am putting myself to any use here,' he replied. After a brief pause to contain his pitch, he continued. 'This friend of mine is working at a restaurant, waiting tables. But the kind of money he makes is more than what even an officer in India takes home. He's been there a few months only and he is already talking about buying his own flat in Delhi… Can you believe that? Moreover, I can't live here anymore. Though he doesn't say it now, but we both know how Papa feels about my living off his money.

'I know how you feel about this, but don't worry; I shall return soon… As soon as I have made enough money,' he added, lovingly patting her on the head. How much of money was enough? Sargam obviously had no answers to a question that had puzzled even the ablest of thinkers for ages. But she could see that Lalit had already made up his mind and any attempts to make him rethink his stance were going to prove futile.

Soon after, through their mother, Lalit broke the news to Lalkrishna as well. Sargam suspected that keeping Lalkrishna in the loop was a ploy germinating from the compulsions facing Lalit rather than a need for conformation. Had it not been for the money he required for paying the agent, he could very well have packed his bags and left without bothering about such niceties.

Lalkrishna agreed to finance his son's endeavour even though it meant taking a loan against his Provident Fund savings. However, his stance with respect to Lalit remained unwavering. The impasse persisted, forcing their mother and sometimes Sargam to relay their messages to and fro. Perhaps if Lalkrishna had any inkling about how long it would be before he got another chance to set eyes on his son, his ego might have considered slipping down a pedestal or two. But destiny's machinations are seldom preceded by a warning.

One fine day Sargam's brother, her only friend in the true sense of the word, bowed out of her life in search of his calling. Sargam barely managed to retain her composure while seeing him off at the airport and once she was back in the house, she locked herself in her room and wept like a child. The sudden realization that Lalit wasn't going to be around anymore was unsettling and frightful. He had been her only source of comfort, the only person she could freely talk to. Her parents, even her mother, had always remained distant and somewhat abstract in their existence while Lalit had been the only living reality. His absence had suddenly turned the home into a house for her – impersonal and objective, as though all its warmth had been pitilessly sucked away.

It was not only Sargam, but even her parents, Lalkrishna included, who were affected by Lalit's departure. The already negligible exchange of words within the walls of the house further diminished as each member appeared to have slipped into a zone of silence of their own.

It wasn't as if Lalit was incommunicado. He had called them upon reaching Paris and since then he had been calling sporadically, about once every couple of months. He had no contact number to give them, he had said, and had instead given them an address where they could write to him.

Sargam however was most perturbed by his constant evasion of questions pertaining to his work or his life in Paris. She was aware that Lalit's status in France was that of an illegal immigrant and she had Googled horrific stories about how such people survived on the streets of Paris. The thought that her brother could be peddling replicas of the Eiffel Tower or something even worse to earn his daily bread was enough to raise the hair at the nape of her neck. But there was no one around to help her battle her inner demons now.

She hadn't even come to terms with her problems when they arose once again in an entirely new avatar. The underlying subject this time was Sargam's marriage.

One evening, after dinner, Lalkrishna invited her to join him on the sofa. The invite had come out of the blue and was a strange one given that Sargam couldn't even recall when her father had last addressed her directly. Barring of course inconsequential bits of chatter like, 'where is the remote?' or 'please get me a glass of water.'

'You know that I will be retiring in a few months…,' he began the prelude to a rather long speech about how it was not only his desire, but also duty to get her married while he was still working.

'Marriage! But I am only in college, with over a year to go before I even graduate,' she wanted to scream, but could not. Perhaps the novelty of speaking one-on-one with Lalkrishna had held her back. She kept listening to the monologue, nodding intermittently, bewildered at the absolute absurdity of the idea. At a time when her friends were busy discussing and thinking about their careers – the right post-graduate course to opt for or the preferred sector for seeking employment – her father wanted to wash off his hands by getting her married. Atrocious!

Lalit's face flashed before her eyes. She was getting a whiff of the despair she had seen him endure, but she did not have the guts to put up a fight like he had. Moreover, as of now marriage was only an idea her father had voiced and there was no immediate danger of its fructification. So, once the monologue concluded, she stepped out of it without voicing her opinion – an act open to be interpreted as tacit concurrence.

Over the following months, the solemnity behind Lalkrishna's words from that evening revealed itself to Sargam. The topic of her marriage seemed to have consumed her parents to a near obsessive degree. Old relatives and friends were excavated from pages of old diaries, contacts were resumed and an all-out search was mounted to find a suitable groom for her.

It was a time-consuming process alright, but every few weeks her parents would have a meeting lined up with the family of a prospective groom for her. It took all of her creativity to come up with plausible excuses to turn them down. Most men she met were not up to the standards she had set for herself. Some were too young and some too old, some too fat and some too short, none that she would ever bring herself to take a fancy to. The two constants however were that all of them belonged to the same caste as her and they came from wealth.

'Money,' Lalkrishna would preach, 'is the most vital ingredient for a happy marriage. You wouldn't want to be slogging all your life washing linen and dishes, would you?' Instantly her mother's image would flash before her eyes. Didn't the description match perfectly with what her life had been? Then perhaps this could be Lalkrishna's way of giving his daughter what he couldn't give to his wife.

But what about her own wants and desires? What if she wanted to earn her own spending money? What if she wanted to build a home herself, instead of becoming an ornament in a palace that her husband had inherited? It wasn't a simple debate, but the fact that she wasn't prepared to get married just as yet conveniently outlined her future course for her. All she needed to do was to deflect the proposals that came her way, and this she managed with remarkable consistency.

Sometimes it would be the frill of social drinking, grossly magnified in her narration, and sometimes a past affair that she would get the credulous prospect to admit, but always an excuse palatable enough for Lalkrishna. And all this while, as she schemed and plotted to wiggle out of yet another marital bid, she would think of her brother and miss him. His struggles had suddenly become much more real to her and she could feel the stifling grip of the very clutches that had eventually compelled him to flee.

She did get to speak to Lalit though, during the random calls he made, but someone – their mother or father – was always around to prevent her from sharing her predicament with him. It was a lonely battle and she had to wage it without the comfort of an ally.

It was with Lalkrishna's retirement that her troubles switched gears. Not that his work had been accounting for much of his time anyway, but even the slight engagement it had offered was suddenly gone. At once Lalkrishna's life had contracted to the confines of the drawing room, more specifically his favourite sofa-chair, and he found himself with even more time and mind-space to devote to Sargam's nuptial cause. If anything, his retirement had made him more determined to get her married and less tolerant of her excuses.

Barely a fortnight after Sargam had successfully evaded a proposal on account of the boy – a lone heir to his family's business – being lesser educated than her own self, Lalkrishna came up with another one. Abhigyan Kukreti, the man in question, was a doctor who had a busy clinic in the heart of South Delhi. Both his parents were no more, Sargam was told, and so, having exhausted all plausible excuses, she had to consent for a private meeting with him. Girl-boy-get-to-know-each-other sorts!

The venue, proposed by Dr. Kukreti, was a coffee shop at one of the prominent city hotels. Though Sargam was now a graduate and had even started working, the glitz and glamour of such establishments was still alien to her. Resultantly, she had a nervous apprehension about the meeting. However, her mother's enthusiasm in getting her ready – draping her in one of the four saris which had now been set aside for such occasions – and the flurry of instructions Lalkrishna bombarded her with, as though he were a regular at such hotels, deprived her of any opportunities to voice them.

Edgy and nervous, she found herself stepping into the intimidating hotel lobby to meet another prospective groom.

Sheepishly, she enquired the directions to the coffee shop from the concierge desk, unsure if she would be able to recognize the man from the photographs. Her fears, however, proved unfounded as Dr. Kukreti emerged from one of the window-side tables and stepped forward to greet her as soon as she entered the arena.

He was a man of sturdy built, not exceptionally tall, but inching above the average, and with a chiselled nose and probing eyes. He wore a brown corduroy jacket atop a pair of denims, lending him a look of casual ease. As he extended a hand towards her, his smile betrayed a pair of perfectly formed dimples.

'You must be Sargam. I am Abhigyan. It's a pleasure to meet you,' he said in a baritone voice before pulling out a chair for her.

He was an impressive man, albeit somewhat elder to her, but Sargam's instincts refused to let go of the nervous shakiness she had felt at his sight. He was charming, no doubt, but perhaps a bit too charming. There was something about him that beggared trust; she couldn't pin-point what. And so, cautiously and non-committedly, she went about the meeting, preferring to listen more and speak less.

Abhigyan was only too glad for the opportunity to talk about his own self, uninterrupted. He told her about the kind of person he thought he was, his work, his life, his recent holidays and other such – all, Sargam thought, to give her a deliberate and measured peek into the riches he could afford to squander. What else could be the point in talking at length about the casinos of Vegas or the animals he had seen during the Masai Mara Safari with a girl who hadn't ever strayed beyond the boundaries of three Indian states?

It was during this elongated introduction that Dr. Kukreti mentioned about his failed marriage. Sargam didn't probe much, given that it was a sensitive matter, but the revelation left her feeling enraged. Her father, who had so vociferously favoured the match, was certain to know about this. Why hadn't he come clean and told her about it then? Or, did he think that it was too trivial a complication to bother her with? Didn't she have the right to know all the facts before making the most important decision of her life? Or, was Lalkrishna simply trying to avoid handing her on a platter another reason to back off?

With great difficulty she checked her emotions, and suppressing the erupting volley of questions, went about listening.

'I am sure you know how pretty you are, even prettier than what I had imagined on the basis of your pictures. I don't know what you think of me, but if you agree to the alliance, I will shower you with all the happiness that money can buy. You deserve to live like a queen and that's what you shall get,' were Abhigyan's parting words, as he gently guided her fingers for a brush with his lips. He had tried to lock his gaze with her, perhaps to give the words more meaning, but in vain. The only thing Sargam could think of then was to get back home, let alone feel the romance her suitor was attempting to create with his words.

She tried using Abhigyan's earlier marriage as a weapon to wiggle out, but Lalkrishna, this time round, appeared in no mood to reason with her.

'He is wealthy, educated, good-looking. What else do you want in a guy?' he countered irritably. 'If he was married earlier, how does that affect you? He is single now, is he not?'

Sargam so wished that she could be more persuasive and obstinate, like Lalit had been, but it just wasn't up her alley. She had to eventually settle for the deal Lalkrishna offered her as a last recourse whereby she could take some time to get to know Abhigyan better before the date for the marriage was fixed. It was a lifeline for her and she latched on to it desperately, leaving it on time to come up with a rescue plan.

Abhigyan proved more persistent than she had imagined, calling her, inviting her out and turning a blind eye to her juvenile attempts at rebuffing him. He was dogged in his pursuit and every now and then, after she had turned him down several times or when her parents insisted, she was compelled to give in. It was during these outings that Dr. Kukreti's true colours became visible to her.

Initially it were his eyes, impudently frank in their appraisal of her, and his jokes and innuendos – often risqué and suggestive – that made her uncomfortable, but with time his attempts became more brazen and indiscreet. The obligatory hug that lasted a moment too long, his eagerness to touch her at the slightest opportunity and the unmistakable residue of lust in his eyes, they were all a dead giveaway of his true motives.

What she abhorred the most though was his continual insistence for her to join him at his place for a round of drinks, and that, when she had repeatedly told him that she was a rigid teetotaller.

'There is a time in life for trying everything. Once we are married, you would anyways be keeping me company when I drink, so why not start now?' he would reason in futility. Sometimes, when in an insistent mood, he would even try to lure her into accepting the offer.

'You know, I tend to get extremely generous while drinking… You must try me out sometime. Who knows I might buy you a diamond pendant or a nice bracelet. You would like that, wouldn't you?'

These arguments made Sargam cringe from within. She felt like a whore, like a prostitute being dangled the promise of riches in lieu of extending sexual favours. This made her hate the man more and more with each passing day, but she had yet not found a way to convey her feelings to her unreceptive parents. She was living in a stalemate, doing what she could do to avoid disturbing the status quo, and hoping that the tides would somehow turn in her favour.

Just the last evening Sargam had met Abhigyan once again. When she had ignored his calls a few times, the rascal had called up her father to help fix the meeting. The meeting had been arranged and Sargam's mother, like the able adherent of Lalkrishna she was, had torn through all of Sargam's excuses, compelling her to see him.

They met at the food-court in one of the malls in Saket, but even the public setting did not discourage Abhigyan from his pursuit. He once again invited her to accompany him to his flat, sparing her a liberal spiel on how she needed to open up to life and embrace the slight joys it held amidst its folds, till Sargam could bear no more. Feigning a headache, she excused herself and came back home. Her mother, as always, was eagerly awaiting her return. Perhaps she eyed these meetings as fragments of hope, each a splinter capable of making her daughter change her mind and give her nod for the marriage. She had only faced disappointment so far and today proved no different. Ignoring her curious looks, Sargam hastily receded to her room.

She was eager to vent out her fury, to speak to someone who could empathize with her, but there weren't too many people around her who met that singular criterion. Geeta, a friend from college, was the only one Sargam had confided in about Dr. Kukreti and her struggles in keeping the man at bay. She thought of giving Geeta a call, but the thought managed to lose itself amid the many that were rummaging through her mind.

It was only the next morning, on her way to the office that Sargam eventually managed to speak to Geeta. There was so much to share and so little time for it. She hadn't even begun to narrate the specifics of her tete-a-tete with Abhigyan when her auto pulled up outside her office. Forced to cut the conversation short, she invited Geeta over to her place the next day. It was a Sunday and she was hoping to spend some lazy time with her friend. Only, she had no way of knowing what the last leg of the day held in store for her. It was a day she wasn't likely to forget in a long, long time – 28th December.

28th December

Sargam emerged from the hotel, as though teetering on the brink of a precipice. Her world had suddenly turned upside down and it wasn't just about the money she had lost. Her dreams, her aspirations of a successful career had all gone kaput over the past few hours. Mr. Ahuja wasn't likely to take his loss lying down. What if he complained to the police? Who would give her a job if she were the subject of an ongoing police investigation?

Listlessly, she surveyed her surroundings. It was dark already, and though there wasn't much traffic on the by-lane leading to the hotel, she could see a chain of restlessly honking vehicles up ahead on the main road. There were a few idle taxis and auto-rickshaws parked on either side of the lane, relying on the hotel to supply them with passengers. She could see the hopeful eyes of drivers curiously surveying her as she stepped past them. Ignoring them, she opted to walk till the main road and give herself the time she desperately needed to get a grip on her senses.

'Madam, auto?' an auto-wallah screamed, craning his neck to ensure that he caught her eye.

Sargam averted her gaze and continued pacing down the path without bothering to voice a refusal. But the slight glimpse of the auto-wallah had got something ticking within her head and she was suddenly inundated with a flurry of fresh thoughts. The packet was in her purse when she had left office. Between then and the time she realized that the packet was missing, it was only in the auto that she had left the purse unattended. Was it possible that the auto-wallah had taken it out?

A part of Sargam was nonetheless sympathetic towards the auto-wallah. He couldn't have taken it. There was no way for him to know that the packet contained money. Why would he take just the packet and not the little bit of her own money or her credit cards from the purse? Moreover, the same guy had been ferrying her for several months and he had given her no reason to doubt his integrity up till now, her compassionate side reasoned.

But, as is so often the case, her empathetic thoughts were consumed by the dread she could feel rumbling within her. On an impulse, she took out her mobile phone and dialled the auto-wallah's number.

'Yes madam,' Sharib's enthusiastic voice greeted her after the third ring.

'Where are you?' she enquired, for the lack of any other opening statement.

'Madam, you asked me not to wait, so I came back. I have already reached home, else I would have come back to pick you up. Why don't you try hailing another auto? It shouldn't be so much of a problem at this hour,' he replied apologetically.

The confidence in the guy's voice betrayed no awareness about the theft, not a sliver of hesitation or reluctance. However, the voice within her head prevented Sargam from giving him any benefit of doubt. 'These guys are master conmen. They know just the right things to say for avoiding the radar of suspicion,' it said to her.

'That's okay. I have called you for another reason,' she began, picking a tone as sombre as she could. 'I called you for the packet that you took out from my purse.'

'Packet…Purse…What are you talking about, madam? I don't understand.'

'Of course you don't understand. Why would you? I am talking about the packet containing one lakh rupees that you stole from my purse. Don't sound so naïve,' she replied. She was trembling with fury and her voice sounded more foreboding than it had ever been. She needed the money back, and desperately. Now that the man had blatantly refused any knowledge of it, her only redemption lay in scaring him into owning up.

'Steal…What are you saying madam?' Sharib returned, sounding offended but cordial. 'Why would I even touch your purse? And when would I do that? The purse was with you on the passenger seat all the time.'

His lack of agitation convinced Sargam that she was on the right track. 'Not all the time, it wasn't. I had left it in the auto when I got out to buy the bouquet. And that's when you helped yourself to the packet, didn't you?'

'Madam, I don't know anything about the packet. I didn't even know that you had left your purse in the auto and not carried it with you. Please trust me.' Sharib was nearly pleading now. To Sargam, this was nothing but another layer of his cleverly crafted defence. She was on the right track, she thought, and if she persisted with her chosen line of questioning, there was a chance that she might infiltrate his resistance.

'I wasn't expecting you to own up at once, so, this doesn't really come as a surprise. But let me tell you that the money belongs to my office, and you have no idea what kind of a man my boss is. He is not going to let you get away with this, that's certain. And with his connections, you will be left with no place to hide in this city at least. So, it is in your best interest that you return the money and forget that this episode ever played out. You have till the night to make up your mind. Come morning and I will be left with no option but to report the theft to my boss as well as the police. You understand?'

Sargam's tone was intimidatingly advisory and she was hoping that she had managed to instill enough fear in Sharib's mind for him to return the packet. This was the only way out of her quandary, she thought.

'Hmm,' Sharib murmured incoherently before disconnecting the call. He hadn't voiced a single word of protest or denial, and this, to Sargam, was a good sign. Maybe he was re-evaluating his decision already. Maybe her words did rattle him enough to compel him to return the money.

Clutching on to the solitary ray of hope, Sargam hailed an auto and blurted out her address for the benefit of the driver. The wait for Sharib's call was going to be a long and excruciating one, she could gather.

◆

Sharib, after disconnecting the phone, plugged it to the charger dangling inertly from the lone plug-point in the room. He then slid against the nearby wall, affixing his gaze to a blotch of peeling paint on the ceiling, unmindful of the tears streaming down his eyes.

A bulb plugged to an unadorned holder was the only source of illumination in the room. In the tawny light emanating from it, one could see signs of near macabre destitution.

Lined up against the two facing walls were mattresses, soiled and torn, with lumps of hardened cotton sticking out in several places. On top of them were two blankets, of cheap and coarse variety, neatly folded and placed on one end. Towards the other end, between the mattresses and the third wall was the only storage space the room's architecture permitted. The space beyond one of the mattresses was occupied by a severely dented metal trunk, while the other comprised a tattered cloth bag bearing the insignia of a known brand of spices.

There was a wooden window in the room and on its slightly protruding ledge was a tidily rolled prayer mat. The fourth wall had a door on one end, a scruffy piece of wood painted in gaudy green that stood ajar, and the corner its other end made up was adorned by a table fan – a dust-laden apparatus with grills that could only be procured from a junk dealer in the present day.

Stepping out of the door, one would land on a small terrace that served as a kitchen cum wash area for the dwelling. Barring the wall from which a plastic tap jutted out and the one framing the room, the terrace had no boundaries or railings, making it an impossible footstall for someone suffering from vertigo. In the only bordered corner of this patch was a kerosene stove, around which a bunch of basic utensils lay scattered. Under the tap was a plastic bucket, cracking at the brim, filled with water. Perhaps the water supply in the building wasn't regular and this was the reserve the inhabitants had to rely on for their needs through the day.

Up ahead was a winding metal stairway that led to the floor below, where, after crossing a corridor lined with common toilets for the building residents, was another flight of stairs. Two more floors to climb down and one would finally emerge from the architectural marvel into the narrow lanes of Nehru Nagar.

Sharib had been living here for nearly three years now, ever since he first came to Delhi. The room had been originally rented by Jamal, the man Sharib had shadowed to the city from his village in Azamgarh district of Uttar Pradesh. Since then, Jamal had moved back to the village, having saved enough to buy a patch of land to raise his family on, and Afzal, another young man from the same village had moved in with Sharib.

Sharib was glad that Afzal had not been around to hear the conversation he had just concluded with 'Madam'. He simply wasn't up to offering the explanations his presence would have warranted.

This was a dark day in Sharib's life, possibly the darkest. Not only had he been accused of theft, a forbidden act, a haraam, according to the tenets of his religion, but even the castles he had quietly and fervidly been erecting within his heart had come crashing down, all at once. All he could see ahead of him, in the abstractions fashioned by the peeling paint, was a gloomy and melancholic darkness. A darkness so befuddling that he was beginning to question the very purpose of his existence.

By now his silent tears had taken the form of a full-blown audible wail and he was crying, like a child in pain, choking, gasping for breath and once again breaking into a relentless sob.

'This can't be happening. I can't let this happen,' he kept telling himself. He had been a fighter all his life and he couldn't bear to watch helplessly as his life crumbled all around him. He needed to do something to resurrect it. Only, he didn't know what.

And then, suddenly, a twinkle appeared in his eyes. It was a thought that had offered him just the leash he had been craving for. Still sniffing, he dabbed his eyes with the back of his hand and reached out for his phone. It was a long shot, alright, but he could not allow the option to slip by. The stakes were high and he had no option but to try all the tricks in the book to win this hand.

Sharib Sheikh

Childhood memories, for most, form a treasure to last an entire lifetime, serving as a retreat in the wake of the constant vagaries of adulthood. Not for Sharib though. His earliest recollections could be termed as anything but pleasurable.

His Abba, Saheb Jan, was a rickshaw-puller in a remote village of Azamgarh district. The village, with a rickety bus running thrice a day through the local market to the district headquarters and back, did not attract many travellers for him to ferry. The odd visitor aside, his customers were mainly women and children visiting the *haat* or the nearby temple, and such visits were by no means regular.

There were days when Saheb Jan, despite having followed the scorching summer sun through its descent, would not find a single customer, and hence, be forced to return home empty handed. If a job of any sort came along where he could earn an assured wage in return for his labour, he would latch on to the opportunity with both hands. In short, the sole purpose of his existence was to somehow feed his family of five. And how he was to do that was a question he set out to answer every morning.

Sharib lived in a small brick-mud hut with his parents and two elder brothers. The brothers, he recalled, were endlessly fighting with each other, much to the chagrin of their Ammi. The reason behind their quarrels was usually food – conflicting claims over the only remaining piece of bread or a bunch of fruits that one of them had discreetly plucked from a nearby orchard. Sharib, being the youngest of the lot, usually got his share without having to wage a battle for it. In that sense, he was lucky.

The hut had no rooms, only a cold mud and dung-smeared floor with a thatched roof and three brick walls. The front end of the dwelling was open, but for the three bamboo sticks to support the roof. There was a small clean patch outside the hut that served as a courtyard of sorts and Saheb Jan had deftly used thorny shrubs and bushes to create a boundary around it. This opening served as a house for chicks that Baudhi, Sharib's Ammi, as she was popularly known around the village, reared.

The poultry, though never enough, provided them with eggs and meat as a sporadic luxurious indulgence. What the family ate for the rest of the days was a function of how much fare Saheb Jan was able to earn. When he could afford flour, lentils and vegetables – not a usual occurrence by any means – the children and their mother feasted heartily, and on other days they had to make do with rice cooked in excess water, served with salt.

Life in the village wasn't easy and Sharib had learnt that at an early age. He hated going to the well, the only source of potable water within a radius of nearly two kilometres, twice every day; and he hated the sight of his father, fatigued and on the brink of collapse, when he returned home in the evenings.

Sharib's fonder memories were of when he would snuggle up to Saheb Jan at night and, massaging his taut forearm and calf muscles with his tiny hands, urge him to tell a bed-time story. Saheb Jan's skin, he distinctly remembered, felt hard and slippery, like a sheet of old plastic, and his eyes would be red with exhaustion. And yet, Sharib's request for a story never went begging. Saheb Jan would conjure for him stories of fairies, princesses and djinns, which he would listen to with rapt attention and dream of later in the night.

Before he started attending the local school with his brothers, Sharib spent most of his days playing with the hens or making clay figurines. He would cringe and sulk, watching his playmates being butchered as Saheb Jan's sharp knife slowly cut through their throats to drain the lifeblood from their veins.

'He is such a softie, a girl almost,' his brothers would tease when he winced at the sight of the *Dhabihah*. His brothers however doted on him and never hesitated in slipping a piece or two of the meat from their own plates to his. It was ironic how Sharib relished the very food, witnessing the preparation of which made him queasy.

He was only in the second grade when both his brothers, Shoaib in fourth grade and Salman in fifth, withdrew from school following a discussion within the household about their further prospects. The school was nothing but a structure erected to influence the political metrics of infrastructure and literacy for the area. Teachers seldom made an appearance except for the last day of the month to collect their pay-checks, and the free books and mid-day meals that the government so vociferously harped about remained just an illusion. Schooling, Saheb Jan felt, was adding no value to his sons and it was about time they began supporting him in running the household. Baudhi didn't have an opinion, and the two boys, if they did have a view, were never asked for it.

Saheb Jan's opinion about education wasn't consistent though. When it came to Sharib, he never recommended his withdrawal from school and the boy was permitted to go about his educational pursuits unabated. Perhaps Shoaib's employment at a tea-stall in the local market and Salman's move to Azamgarh town to work as a domestic help in a household with its roots tracing back to an affluent family from the village had given him the necessary provisions to alter his views.

During his growing up years, Sharib didn't have many friends. He was essentially a loner and preferred being in the company of his own thoughts to the aimless cavorting other kids his age liked to indulge in. Of course, there was Ameena, a girl from the neighbourhood that Sharib would walk to school and back with. However, as soon as she stepped into her early teens, her folks too promptly pulled her out of school.

'Where will I find a suitable boy to marry her if she studies too much? More than half the boys in the village have anyway dropped out of school much before she has. Moreover, it is about time she started learning the nuances of running a household,' her father had confided in Saheb Jan about the reasons behind Ameena's unceremonious exit from the realms of formal learning.

Ameena however remained a part Sharib's life for the next few years. She would visit him upon his return from school and pester him to tell her about the lessons he had learnt or about their common acquaintances – teachers and students alike. Her curiosity was palpable. She was like a child who had been pulled out of the enchanted forest much before her fascination with the surroundings had worn out. But amazingly, she never complained. Sharib had not once heard her grumble about not being able to attend school or even express a desire to go back. Her muted conciliation made Sharib realize the value of all that he was blessed with and he swore to himself that he would not abandon his quest for education for as long as he could help.

Their tryst proved short-lived though; with time, Sharib began to feel an awkward unease creeping between them. It wasn't as if he had developed a dislike for Ameena. It was just that the features distinguishing their gender were becoming more definite and apparent with each passing day. An accidental brush of the hand or a thoughtlessly uttered word had suddenly acquired dimensions that were hitherto alien to them, and this discomfited him immensely.

He began to avoid her, excusing himself whenever the two were alone and speaking to the bare minimum when in the company of others. It was just a matter of time that Ameena became aware of the insinuation and ceased her efforts to seek his company. She disengaged from his life without uttering a single word of protest, once again, accepting the dictates of destiny with demurely downcast eyes.

It was much later, after Sharib had been accorded his bachelor's degree by the University, when Ameena stepped into his life for the second time. And this time it wasn't just a childish intrusion but a calibrated prospecting for companionship of a lifetime. It was through Saheb Jan that Sharib learnt about the marriage proposal Ameena's Abba had put forth on behalf of his daughter. Saheb Jan had animatedly broken the news to his wife, like a peddler having managed to sell his last and minutely defective ware, but to Sharib the prospect had sounded ever so daunting and nearly obnoxious.

How could he marry a girl he hadn't set his eyes on for the past several years and whose last reminiscences he had were of when she wore her hair in a pair of immaculate ponytails? Was his life going to tread the same path as his brothers' – get married, reproduce, and live a life of obscurity and insignificance? The answer was quick to pop-up within his head, but the task of voicing it in front of his father proved beyond his faculties.

It was at this decisive juncture that he happened to meet Jamal. Jamal, like many other youngsters from the region had moved to Delhi in search of a livelihood and was visiting his family for Eid.

When Salman had introduced them at the local mosque, Sharib couldn't help but notice the fine embroidery on his kurta and the rich texture of its fabric. It was of a quality, and perhaps price, that the local garment shops couldn't even dream of stocking. Even his skull-cap – in green velvet with golden thread work – was unlike any that Sharib had seen.

It weren't just his adornments, Jamal's accent too was different – refined, just like that of the actors on television. He had big-city anecdotes to share on just about everything and consequently was thronged by a bunch of eager and fascinated villagers, Sharib included. In Jamal and his narratives Sharib could see unblemished images of the blurry visions he had been nurturing in private about his own life. Jamal was just the escape Sharib needed to prevent his life from shaping in the same mould that had fashioned Salman's and Shoaib's.

Over the next few days, till Jamal's vacation lasted, Sharib would visit him every day, questioning and quizzing him about his life in Delhi. He learnt that Jamal plied a rented auto rickshaw in the city and comfortably pocketed between 300 and 500 rupees a day – a sum of money that usually took Saheb Jan over a fortnight to put together. The arrangement was simple – the daily rental he had to pay for the vehicle to its owner was fixed, and any money he made over and above that and the gas he had used up was for him to keep.

'The Seth whose auto I drive owns more than a dozen of them. If you are interested, I could put in a word for you,' sensing his enthusiasm, Jamal once remarked. It was this remark that proved a turning point in Sharib's life. A few days later, he found himself seated next to Jamal on the rickety state-transport bus heading to Lucknow, from where they were to board a train to Delhi.

His brothers expectedly, and surprisingly his father too, expressed their unequivocal support for his enterprise. Baudhi was the only one he found nursing a hint of sadness in her eyes at his departure, but she was a mother and which mother is not aggrieved by an impending separation with her offspring? An obvious casualty of the episode was the proposal for his marriage which slipped out of the frame inconspicuously and Sharib could only thank his stars for it.

The city of Delhi didn't exactly match up to the picture Sharib had been painting. Although Jamal left no stone unturned to help him settle down – inviting him to share his own accommodation, taking him on long auto rides to familiarize him with the city roads and its ways and introducing him to the Seth who, on Jamal's surety, agreed to rent him one of his vehicles – Sharib couldn't check his thoughts from drifting homewards.

The confines of his cramped room and the sea of humanity enveloping him wherever he went made the tiny village he had left behind seem like a sprawling expanse. He longed to run amok on the dusty village roads and when tired, to return to his meagre, but warm and welcoming house. He missed his father, his brothers and most of all, his mother. But despite his misgivings about the city, he knew that the dice had been rolled and if he had to challenge his destiny, the arena could be no other.

It was proving a time-taking exercise, adjusting to life in the big city. Back in Azamgarh, greasing a few palms had ensured that he got his driver's license without even appearing for a test, but it was on the streets of Delhi that Sharib's driving skills were being put to test day in and day out. The maze of traffic signals crowding every intersection, the torrent of metallic monsters aggressively carving their path amid the chaos and the labyrinth of streets and alleys that made up the city were all but refutations to his claim of belongingness. He was an outsider and in his head he was certain that he was always going to remain one.

There was only one reason for him to endure this madness – money – and he put his heart and soul behind making as much of it as he could. He would work sixteen hour shifts, scouting the Delhi streets for passengers to be ferried to just about anywhere within the frontiers outlined by the vehicle's permit, and return home only when exhaustion made it impossible for him to carry on. He had set himself a personal target of buying his own auto rickshaw within a span of two years, a goal he could not share even with Jamal as he was still reliant on Seth ji's fleet, despite having spent four good years in the city.

Jamal, he knew, wanted to eventually return to the village and had been saving for a patch of land he could live off for the rest of his life. 'Nothing wrong with that,' Sharib would muse in private, 'but this isn't what I left my house for. Once I buy my own auto, I will save on the rent and consequently my earnings will nearly double. It will take me another year to buy a second one, which I can rent out, and with the combined income of both vehicles it will take me about five to seven years to buy a small flat of my own.' His plans were ambitious. He wanted to rescue Saheb Jan and Baudhi from their dreary existence in the village. He wanted to give them a better life and it was this larger goal that he was striving towards.

Only, Sharib had no way of assessing Jamal's sincerity towards his stated objective or how close he was to accomplishing it. So, it came as a shock when one evening Jamal confided in him about his readiness to return home. Expectedly, Jamal was excited. Sharib on the other hand was left to recommence without the company of his friend and mentor, an unnerving prospect by all means.

Keeping his anxiety at bay wasn't easy, but the last thing Sharib wanted was to add even a dash of unpleasantness to Jamal's unrepressed joy. So, he took some time off work and opted to accompany his friend back to the village. Nearly eight months had passed since the duo had boarded the train to Delhi, and the longing to see his parents, his brothers, albeit not menacing, had been growing constantly somewhere deep within him. Before they departed, Sharib even took out time to visit the Lajpat Nagar market and pick up presents for everyone.

The one person he missed buying a gift for was Ameena, and rightfully so, for he had hardly even thought about her since his departure from the village. Therefore it came as a surprise when, along with his family members, he found Ameena waiting to welcome him. Perhaps Saheb Jan or one of his brothers hadn't been particularly discreet about his itinerary and she had got wind of his arrival, he presumed.

A commotion of sorts ensued as soon as he entered the house, giving him just the opportunity he needed to mask his surprise. He greeted everyone, wiping the tears streaming down Baudhi's eyes with his palms and even sparing a nonchalant smile for Ameena, before settling down on a cane stool. Others, barring his younger sister-in-law who rushed to boil some tea for everyone, surrounded him just like he had seen the village kids surround the candy-man, utterly eager and impatient.

Between them they had a barrage of questions for him - about the city and his life there – and he answered each one decoratively, doing all he could to satisfy their collective curiosity. Ameena was the only one who didn't have anything to ask, but he knew that her eyes had not left him even for a fraction of a second. It was almost intrusive, her penetrative gaze, and Sharib was glad when Baudhi, by way of a signal she thought to be subtle, summoned him. Feigning an apologetic grin he got up and followed her outside the hut.

'Shoaib says you have come only for two days?' she said, catching his gaze.

'Yes Ammi, I can't be absent for long. Seth ji won't keep the auto idle for too many days. He will enlist another driver and that won't auger well for me.'

She hummed thoughtfully before opening her mouth once again. 'Cooking your own meals after a hard day's work – and I am not even sure how well you would be faring – aren't you tired of living the life of a hermit? Don't you think it's time that you gave marriage a serious thought?'

Alarm bells had begun to ring within his head, but Sharib could do little to avoid the dialogue now. 'Living in Delhi is expensive, Ammi. I am still trying to find my footing there. As soon as I begin to earn enough to fend for two people, I will think about it.'

'This girl, Ameena,' Baudhi continued as if she hadn't heard a word he had uttered, 'she is a nice girl. Even while you were away, she had been visiting us regularly, doing little chores around the house to make herself useful. But I have seen much more of life than she has; she can't fool me. The only reason she has been coming here is you, the hope of catching any news, any piece of information about you. She really loves you and I think she will make the perfect bride for you.'

Sharib stood stunned, staring uncertainly at his mother. Her objective was apparent and understandable, but it was the word she had used – Love – that left him dumbfounded. The word was incongruous to the image of hers he had grown up with. Sharib had never imagined that Baudhi would even be aware of the concept of love, the girl-boy variety, let alone talk to him about it. 'I will give it a thought, Ammi,' was all he was able to mutter.

For the remainder of his short stay, he avoided situations that could give his mother another chance at having a go at him. He remained out of the house mostly, surrounded by aspiring youngsters who, motivated by Jamal's success story, were only too eager to accompany Sharib to Delhi. It was around this time that he met Afzal, a promising young man whom he consented to take under his aegis.

Upon his return to the city, Sharib once again submerged himself in work, eating and sleeping his dream of owning an auto rickshaw one day. As is often the case, a dream pursued with tenacity and passion gradually slithers into the realms of reality. It took him nineteen months – five months ahead of his original target – to save enough to be able to purchase a second-hand auto rickshaw.

His exultation, as he drove his newly-acquired vehicle to the Nehru Nagar tenement, was unparalleled. He felt like a groom returning home with his newlywed bride, upbeat and cheerful. Dusty roads, the constantly honking vehicles he swerved past and the cantankerous kids who had made the streets their playground – to him, they all appeared to be partakers of his joy. Little did he know that the auto was but a harbinger to another, much more significant, turn his life was all set to take.

The next morning, after indulgently scrubbing and wiping the vehicle, Sharib set out to earn his first fare as an owner-driver. He drove up to the Ring Road and parked the vehicle on a by-lane adjacent to a group of residential buildings. Office goers from the nearby buildings, he knew, offered a catchment of passengers to ferry.

The wait didn't prove long. About seven minutes would have passed when a girl emerged from one of the complexes and asked him if he would drop her to Okhla. Sharib obliged. He didn't pay much attention to the passenger then. She was just another indifferent office-goer, looking for a ride to take her to her workplace. But later in the evening, when he returned to his room and counted his booty, he realized that it had been his most commercially productive day since he had started plying an auto. Maybe it had something to do with the girl, his first passenger for the day. Sharib wasn't particularly superstitious, but he couldn't shake away this thought till sleep took control of his tired limbs and mind.

Next day, around the same time, Sharib parked his auto at the same spot. It was a long shot alright, but somewhere deep within was a hope that his passenger of the previous morning would show up once again. And when he saw the girl making for his auto in graceful strides, his heart leapt at the sight. The nip of joy he experienced was inexplicable and he found himself unable to take his eyes away from her.

'Madam, do you go to office at the same time every day?' he ended up asking as soon as she was seated. The words had slipped out of their own volition and he could only bite his tongue and curse under his breath now. The girl had only hailed his auto twice. For all he knew, she could be travelling to Okhla temporarily, or even if she did take the same route daily, the auto could have been a temporary arrangement necessitated by a car-breakdown or something. He had obviously spoken too soon, the voice in his head, one that belonged to a shy villager, told him.

'Yes, I do,' she said. 'And if you are okay to ferry me to work and back daily, we could look at an arrangement of some sort.'

He couldn't believe his ears first, but when the words sank in, he let out a sigh of relief. She continued speaking, something arithmetical about the average fares and how much they would add up to for an entire month, but Sharib was beyond listening now. His wish had been granted and all he was now focusing on was to keep the satisfied grin from showing on his face.

The routine began, Sharib meeting her at the same place six mornings a week and dropping her at the office in Okhla, and in the evenings, ferrying her back home from work. It was on the third day of their arrangement that he learnt her name – Sargam. That evening, on not being able to locate the auto, she had called him and introduced herself using her name. Sharib, forced by the evening congestion to park a little ahead of his regular place, had seen 'Madam' flashing on his cellphone screen and accepted the call in an animated haste. 'Sargam here,' she had said. Her chiming voice ran though his circuits like a mild electrical current, bringing his senses to rapt attention. Despite her mildly hassled tone, she sounded just as she always did – tender and poised. She didn't really have to introduce herself. Even if he didn't have her number stored, Sharib would have recognized her with the first words she uttered.

Sharib, of whatever he had seen of the girls in Delhi, didn't hold them in particularly high esteem. His small-town antecedents lent him a disparaging view of the kind of clothes they wore, the manner in which they walked and talked, and the way he saw them mingling with the menfolk. They were simply 'too fast' by his standards. But Sargam was different. She was quite unlike any of the other Delhi girls that he had come across. Not to say that he had observed too many girls at such close quarters, but that notwithstanding, Sargam was certainly a class apart.

She was soft spoken and yet assertive, ambitious and yet grounded to her roots, and most of all, she was attractive in an extremely pleasant sort of a way. This wasn't just his first impression of her. It was a perception that had shaped over several weeks of observing her, listening to telephonic conversations she carried out from the back seat of the auto and the few words that were sporadically exchanged between them. She had everything that a girl might need to keep her man happy.

It began with random thoughts about her sprouting at the strangest of times – when he was haggling with a passenger or when he was standing in the long queue outside a gas station or even when he had snuggled up in his bed for the night. He didn't resist them initially, for they had a peculiarly soothing effect on him. His lips would invariably curl up in a smile the moment his mind drifted towards Sargam.

The words she had spoken would repeat themselves within his head and her images that his eyes had captured would start playing incessantly like reruns of television soaps. Her thoughts never came accompanied by a shower of petals or with a musician playing the violin in the background, but when the frequency of their occurrence reached alarming proportions, the precariousness of the situation dawned upon Sharib.

It was love. He, an auto rickshaw driver, had fallen in love with one of his passengers – a happening so bizarre that it merited coverage by one of those bearded, overenthusiastic anchors on certain 24-hour news channels. The very sound of this was atrocious even to Sharib. Sargam and he were poles apart, with no common ground between them. She was educated and employed, and he, a mere auto driver. And not to forget, she was a Hindu and he a devout Muslim.

A part of him was desirous of quelling his misplaced obsession, but his baser self was already gamboling off into the realms of happy speculation. What if she had similar feelings for him? She had to get married to someone, so why not him? He was building wish-castles, he knew, but his lovelorn heart had learnt to leap into a world of fantasies and there was no holding back now. Perhaps the inappropriateness of his adventure had dawned upon him a tad bit late.

However, he knew better than to express his feelings to the subject of his affection. At Sargam's sight, the two warring factions within him reached some sort of a compromise that allowed his pragmatic side to seize control. He would be happy stealing sporadic glances at her through the rear view mirror and exchanging just enough words to belie suspicion. If she did become aware of his designs, there was every chance that she would terminate their arrangement and that, to him, was a risk not worth taking.

Life, with its glorious uncertainties, was ebbing along when the news of Saheb Jan's ill health took him back to his village once again. Of course he remembered to inform Sargam of his impending absence in advance.

What had been conveyed to Sharib as a terminal illness of some sort turned out to be only a severe bout of pneumonia. Saheb Jan remained bed-ridden and frail, but the diagnosis did well to rekindle the family's dwindling spirits.

To Baudhi, the scare provided just the excuse she had been waiting for. She quickly changed tracks and got behind getting Sharib married with a renewed vigour. With much effort he was able to thwart her offensives till the day he woke up from his afternoon siesta to find the house startlingly empty. It was only after a few minutes that he spotted the meek figure of Ameena sitting on a plank of wood near the gas stove.

'Some tea?' she called out upon catching his eye.

A masterstroke, he mused. 'Where are the others?' he quizzed, totally ignoring her question.

'They have gone to see Rubina's newborn. Baudhi asked me to look after the house in her absence,' she replied imperturbably. 'What nonsense,' he wanted to scream. Rubina, a girl from the neighbourhood, had delivered a perfectly healthy baby boy about a week back, if not more. Hell, the child was born even before Sharib had come home. Why the sudden urge to see him now?

By now Ameena had poured some water into a glass and was standing at his bedside, proffering it. He accepted the glass and began sipping from it, evading her piercing gaze as he did so. It was a much needed distraction for him to regain his bearings and mount a counteroffensive.

'Is there someone else in the city?' she shot out suddenly. The bluntness of the question and the sharpness of her voice nearly made him choke. He even spilled some of the water on his shirt. She stood motionless as he wiped the wetness, first off his chin then the shirt.

'What do you mean?' he eventually muttered.

'You know perfectly well what I mean. Our families have been discussing our marriage for months, but you, for some reason, have been running away from it. So, is there some other girl in the city that you wish to wed?'

'It's nothing like that. Just that the city is an expensive place and I can't think of having a family with the kind of money I make,' he responded. He rued the words as soon as they came out. They sounded as lame as a child giving excuses to skip school.

'If that's the only problem, we can deal with it. You wouldn't need to spend a penny on me. I will find myself some work there and fend for myself,' she retorted, shredding his argument to bits.

'You don't understand...,' was all he could say. There was no way he could tell her that he was in love with one of his passengers, and that the girl in question wasn't even aware of his feelings. Even if he ignored the silliness of the situation for once, Ameena was sure to relay the news to his mother, her co-conspirator, and all hell would break loose then. Who is the girl? What is the family like? Is she a Shia or a Sunni? He didn't have the answers to most questions that would be raised, and the ones he had, he wasn't in a position to voice.

Ameena meanwhile, like a soldier on a mission, was determined to take the dialogue to its fruition. Sharib's diversionary tactics, the ones that had worked wonders with Baudhi, did nothing to dent her resolve. She had answers to every excuse he thought up and he, in turn, was struggling to counter her with logic and rationality.

'Why don't you get it? I can't get married to you. Why don't you find yourself another man instead? I am sure there are plenty of worthy men here in the village,' he finally snapped in frustration.

'Oh, so that's what this is about? You have become a Dilli-wala now and you think a village girl is not good enough for you? But this…this…committing to marriage and then walking out of it at will must be acceptable in your city, but not here. Since the day your Abba said yes to our alliance, I have only thought of you as my husband and no one else. If I am ever going to get married, it will be with you and only you. I am not going to let you walk out on me so easily,' she said before storming out of the house. Sharib sat there transfixed, taken aback by this facet of a girl he had supposedly known for many-many years.

Ameena's outburst had been shocking and he had a hard time explaining to Baudhi about what he had said to upset the girl to such a degree. In a few days it was time for him to return to Delhi and he was glad to find an escape route. The episode and its bitter aftertaste would be left behind and he would return to the life that he was solely and totally in charge of, or so he presumed.

In less than a fortnight of returning from the village, Sharib learnt from his brother that Ameena too was moving to Delhi. Several families from villages around Azamgarh were settled in Nehru Nagar, and one of them, Sharib knew, was distantly related to her family. That is where she intended to put up – within striking distance of him. Her words were not going to remain a hollow threat after all.

True to the information, Ameena landed up in the city soon after. She came to pay him a visit the very day she arrived. Her conduct was cordial, as if the altercation back in the village had never actually happened, and she even got him a tiffin-full of home cooked Biryani. Sharib played along as well, making small talk about the village and how different it was to be in the city, before walking her back to her relatives' quarters.

Her first visit however, was only a precursor to what was soon to become a routine. Minutes after Sharib would reach home, Ameena would descend, carrying with her a brimming tiffin box, as though she had been staking him out. He had little to complain with regard to the tiffin, but Ameena's continual presence started becoming a source of annoyance for him. He could no longer sit in peace and think about Sargam, an act he had come to relish somewhere along the way. The fact that he knew the ulterior motive behind her visits made it only worse. Her presence was like an intrusion into the secret world he had conjured for Sargam and himself.

As a subtle expression of his displeasure, he stopped walking her back when she returned, but this didn't prove enough of a deterrent. Her visits continued unabated. He told himself that the arrangement was only temporary and that she would soon see the futility behind her efforts and return home. But once again he was to be proven wrong.

One evening, Ameena casually informed him that she had found a job. Ignoring the call of courtesy and his own curiosity, Sharib refrained from probing much into it. The signals he sent out to her had to be congruent and if he expressed interest in any aspect of her life, including her newfound job, it ran the risk of being misconstrued. So, all he learnt was that she, with the help of her relatives, had enlisted with a utility services company, who in turn had stationed her at a doctor's clinic somewhere in South Extension. She would be working eight-hour shifts as a cleaner. 'It is at least better than working as a domestic help in multiple households,' Sharib thought, but once again avoided voicing his opinion.

The job meant that Ameena wasn't leaving Delhi anytime soon. Another obvious implication was that she could no longer visit him every day and Sharib could only be glad for the respite it offered.

He had heard tales about the strangeness of love, mostly accepting them with a pinch of distrust, but he was now suffering in its throes himself. The futility of his affection for Sargam was not unknown to him, and yet detachment wasn't even a remote consideration. Driving her from Srinivaspuri to Okhla and back had become the highlight of his life – the moments he would live for, and live on for the rest of his waking hours. And his heart, which was once fuelled by ambition and a strong will to make something of his life, was happy to let him remain adrift in the vagueness of his fantasies.

Today morning had been no different. He had met her at the designated spot and driven her to office. She had seemed somewhat distressed he thought – a deduction made from eavesdropping on the telephonic conversation that had kept her occupied for better part of the journey. He was concerned, but not for long. Soon the rigor of negotiating the Delhi traffic consumed him and it was only towards the evening, when he had to go back to pick her, that she surfaced in his thoughts once again. It had been a busy day and although he hadn't yet counted his earnings, he was certain that the daily average had been breached some time back.

'I need to go to the Park hotel today,' she said, sliding into the backseat. 'And if there is a florist somewhere along the way, I need a couple of minutes there as well.'

The detour wasn't a problem. It only meant that he would remain in her proximity for that much longer. However, upon reaching the hotel, when she unexpectedly offered to settle the fare, Sharib's hopes suddenly came crashing down. He tried to cling on to the chance by offering to wait till her work was done, but Sargam was quick to turn down the offer. Not meaning to sound overly eager, he retreated demurely and sputtered back to Nehru Nagar in his auto.

If he thought that the day had ended for him, he was wrong. It still had a final twist concealed within its folds, one that would ensure that the date – 28th December – remained etched on Sharib's heart and soul for a long-long time.

28th December

'You got late today?' Lalkrishna's voice greeted Sargam as soon as she stepped inside the house. She spared him a glance, but could only catch the back of his head. He was glued to the television set. She looked at her mother who was bolting the door behind her, shrugged, and made for her room.

'Abhigyan had called,' she heard his voice once again. She paused and looked back, only to find him focused on the television screen. The drama unfolding on TV – a heavily decked up mother-in-law screaming her guts out on an equally bedizened, but sombre looking daughter-in-law – was perhaps too compelling for him to even look at his daughter while addressing her.

'Mummy, I need to finish some office work and it might take a bit of time. Don't wait for me over dinner. Just leave my plate on the table and I will have it once I am done,' she instructed, before entering her room and bolting it from inside. Lalkrishna's comment didn't deserve a response and she wasn't in a particularly conversational mood anyway.

Dumping her handbag on the bed, she opened the window and slumped down on the nearby cane chair. It was a chilly night and the breeze brushing against her face felt refreshing. Instinctively, she shut her eyes and began tracing the events since she had come in possession of the envelope. Once, twice, thrice, she repeated the sequence in her head, focusing on every slight detail, but could not come up with any other plausible explanation for its disappearance.

'It has to be the auto driver. No one else could have taken it,' she nearly muttered. She then began replaying the conversation she had had with Sharib, word by word. The man had been outright in his denial. What were the chances that he would now own up to the theft? She had done a reasonable job of intimidating him, she thought, but was it going to prove enough? Maybe she shouldn't have called him in such haste. She could have given herself a bit of time to plan her arguments better. But the damage was done now and all she could do was wait and hope for the best.

The question however was whether she could afford to sit tight and do nothing about the situation. What if the auto driver did not own up? She had to make good the money by the coming Monday anyhow. Should she approach the police? They surely would know how to get the money back from Sharib. Had it been a smaller sum, she could have considered paying it out of her own savings, but one lakh rupees was a considerable amount. Almost five times the balance in her savings account.

She sat grappling with these thoughts for a long time, staring blankly into space till her eyes refused to stay ajar, and then, shut them momentarily. Her body appeared sluggish, but her mind was working at a frantic pace – was there someplace she could get the money from? Borrow maybe? Lalkrishna? Could she borrow the money from her father?

The chance, she knew, was bleak, but she could not allow any alternative to be dropped without being given its due consideration. Lalkrishna had spent beyond his means for Lalit's departure to France. She wasn't aware of the exact financial ramifications, but even now she would catch occasional snippets of worried exchanges between her father and mother which told her that all wasn't hunky-dory. In all probability, Lalkrishna wasn't left with the kind of money she needed.

And even if he did have the money, would he be willing to part with it? The only reason her story sounded plausible to her was that she was in the midst of it. Would it prove as simple for Lalkrishna to believe her? If he did believe her, would he also understand the gravity of her situation? He would probably suggest that since Sargam hadn't deliberately lost the money, she should tell her boss just that and leave him to figure out methods for its recovery. Lalkrishna had a righteous streak that was known to show up at the most inopportune times, and a demand for money to cover her office's loss would be just the trigger it needed.

His retirement, and perhaps the investment he had made behind Lalit, had made Lalkrishna overly sensitive to matters concerning money. He had taken to spending every rupee as if it were his last. The fact that he had all the time at hand to deliberate over his expenses, even the most regular ones, didn't help either. Maybe it was the insecurity of a lifetime of steady salary income suddenly shrinking to an insignificant pension, but given Sargam's present dilemma, it only spelt futility and hopelessness.

She eventually retreated to the bed, wishing that her disturbing thoughts wouldn't shadow her, but only in vain. Her restlessness was deep-rooted and the ploy of blinding herself to the situation wasn't going to work. Inadvertently, her mind kept charting out possible escape routes for her, some particularly obnoxious ones, until her body refused to cooperate and slipped into slumber.

◆

Dr. Kukreti took the glass to his mouth one last time, took a long swig to empty its contents and returned it to the table with a thud. Wiping his lips with the back of his hand, he held the handrails of the sofa and pushed himself up.

It was late in the night. He tried peering at the wall-clock, hoping that it would reveal its blurry hands to him. It didn't. After letting out an exasperated sigh, he began his quavering walk towards the bedroom.

It was a cosy apartment with adornments bespeaking money. There was a Tagore original on one wall and facing it was a Hussain original print. There were several wooden and metal artefacts, most, by the looks of them, picked from markets in Eastern Europe and Middle East. Tawny light from the crystal chandelier bathed the room, giving it a rich golden glow.

Abhigyan's fingers, as he crossed the passage, found a switch to push the house into complete darkness. The bedroom door was already ajar. Without bothering to switch on the lights, he aimed for the bed and allowed his body to crash down, face first.

It had been a busy and eventful day for him. Patients had flocked his clinic as though the city was in the grip of some gastrointestinal epidemic. It was a Saturday, one of the two days in the week that he didn't go to the hospital and focused wholly on his practice. He was engaged with a prominent hospital as a visiting gastroenterologist and this not only added to his reputation as a doctor, but also acted as a source for him to acquire new patients for his clinic.

Dr. Kukreti had learnt early that he could either stick to the customary medical oath of being guided by the interest of his patients at all times and lead an ordinary life; or he could let economics take over and reap the rewards he deserved for having spent seven years of his life in the company of books and lab equipment. It wasn't much of a choice as far as he was concerned.

Therefore, whenever he could, he would lure patients he met at the hospital's Out Patients Department (OPD) to his own clinic. The patients, hardly in a position to turn down a suggestion by the man in whose hands their lives rested, would usually oblige, raking in the mullah for Dr. Kukreti. 'It is a win-win situation,' he would tell himself on the rare occasions that his conscience took a turn in its slumber. 'Not only will they receive better care and attention at my clinic, but I am also saving them a lot of money.'

His reasons weren't entirely unfounded either. The hospital, with its disproportionately higher fixed costs, could not match Dr. Kukreti's cost of treatment. Also, since most specialists had similar arrangements with the hospital as Dr. Kukreti, they were not always available to see patients. Consequently, in case of emergencies, patients were forced to meet whichever doctor happened to be available and not necessarily the one they had met in the past. On the other hand, by visiting the doctor's clinic instead, the patients were assured the sole supervision of Dr. Kukreti, emergency or no emergency.

Meanwhile, the hospital authorities, in their ever-frenzied existence, never got around to missing a few OPD patients who had once been in the need for sustained or expensive treatments. It was just their roster undergoing its organic cleansing and no one had the inclination or the intent to scrutinize it. The doctor's little arrangement had therefore been working just fine.

Even today, two of the patients he had baited at the hospital had visited him at the clinic. One was an elderly businessman with no particular ailment other than his paranoia. He was one of those who believed that regularly visiting a doctor and spending on expensive medication was but the surest path to good health. In him Dr. Kukreti saw the opportunity of prescribing expensive tonics and supplements and in the bargain placating the pharmaceutical companies he was known to be aligned with. Of course the promise of regular consultation charges wasn't a bad thing either.

The second case was a little more complicated. The patient had undergone an operation for gallbladder removal at a government hospital and in the bargain had suffered an injury to her bile duct. She was an elderly lady in her fifties and it was her son who had got her to the hospital to see Dr. Kukreti. The diagnosis was clear and the solution, a complex and major corrective surgery.

To begin with, Abhigyan hadn't even bothered recommending his clinic to them. The operation was complex and although his clinic was well-equipped, he felt more comfortable dealing with such cases at the hospital instead. Moreover, the clinic couldn't accommodate overnight patients and the likelihood that the lady would be in a position to head home the very day she was operated upon was remote. Besides, by the looks of it, neither the patient nor her son appeared adequately funded to arouse his interest.

Although the symptoms were pretty precise when Abhigyan first saw the patient, he prescribed an interim medication and a couple of tests for the sake of diagnostic accuracy. In three days' time, the son was back with the test reports, confirming the doctor's suspicions and worse. The injury was acute, and with each passing day, the risk of internal infections was mounting. The patient needed urgent surgical intervention, despite which the threat to her life couldn't be entirely negated.

Abhigyan was glad that it was the son and not the patient herself who sat facing him. Despite a considerably long career in medicine, he hadn't yet mastered the art of professionally and impersonally delivering such news. It pained him to watch his patients lose hope, right up to the last sliver, as the profundity of his words hit them. Instead, passing on the information to a relative was just a tad bit better. Therefore, without mincing his words, Abhigyan had shared his diagnosis and recommended treatment with the man sitting across the table.

'Time,' he added, 'is of utmost importance. The longer you postpone the operation, the bleaker its chances of succeeding. Ideally you should get her admitted to the hospital right away and block the first available slot in the O.T.'

The man sat still for a few seconds, blankly holding the doctor's gaze as though he were trying to assimilate the words he had heard. Then suddenly he got up from the chair and folded his hands. 'I will do everything I can Doctor Saheb, but please save my mother. Please don't let her die. She is all that I have in this world,' he said with a quiver in his voice that made Abhigyan's heart cringe.

The doctor could only console him, and that he did, before directing him to the hospital reception for completing the admission formalities. However, within a matter of minutes the man barged into Abhigyan's chamber once again. He looked furious and aghast.

'They are saying that the operation will cost upwards of three lakh rupees…,' he said, allowing his words to tail. Abhigyan sat waiting for him to complete his statement, but nothing followed. He stood there gaping, waiting to hear from the doctor instead. It was as though he expected Abhigyan to burst out laughing at the outrageousness of what the man at the reception had said to him. He had come to the hospital for his mother's treatment, not to buy the building itself.

The estimate was accurate. Abhigyan knew that a surgery of such nature would indeed cost over three lakh rupees, but explaining the commerce to an unfortunate son vying for his mother's life was an altogether different matter.

An uncomfortable exchange ensued, rationality pitted against desperate imploration, and in the heat of the moment, Abhigyan ended up committing to the procedure for a quarter of the amount. This was significantly lower than what he charged his patients for much simpler treatments at his clinic, but it was one of those rare occasions when he had allowed his heart to define the terms. Moreover, he would make a profit even at the price he had quoted, albeit only a marginal one.

'No other doctor in the city will touch this case for such a sum. Just that the operation will have to be conducted at my clinic and you will need to make necessary arrangements to take the patient home within a few hours of it. Of course, I will be available on call in case any unforeseen complication arises, but this is a risk you need be cognizant of.... And, don't delay it. Make sure that you complete the formalities tomorrow itself so that the surgery can happen on Saturday.'

Abhigyan felt wonderful watching the grateful man leave his chamber. It wasn't a feeling he was accustomed to and it was perhaps the newness of the experience that made it an even more satiating one.

The man did not return the next day. However, the day after, which was today, he materialized at the clinic and deposited the entire fees in advance. The operation was now scheduled for Monday, the day after. This wasn't a routine procedure for Abhigyan and he was somewhat nervous about having taken it up, but that didn't take away from the feeling of fulfilment his decision had aroused within him. There also was another reason behind his feeling of contentment, a more pragmatic one relatively. His clinic had grossed a collection of over two-and-a-half lakh rupees for the day, an enviable sum for any private practitioner in the city, and certainly his personal best.

The rush of patients had forced him to stay in the clinic beyond his usual hours. When he was done examining them, he slumped down on his easy-chair and glanced through the figures on his laptop. The day's booty had overshot his best expectations by a mile. He shut his eyes to soak in the flavour of success and inadvertently his lips curled into a smile.

He felt a desperate need to celebrate, to share his success with someone who would appreciate it for what it was – a remarkable feat. And suddenly he felt overpowered by a powerful rush of gloom. Not a name to fit the simple criteria came to his mind. Despite his frantic schedule, he had managed to retain a few friends in his life, but they were all family men now and beckoning them at this hour wasn't likely to yield favourable results. As for family, he had none.

The loneliness was overwhelming, dwarfing all his material achievements instantly, and then, like an oasis in the desert, a face suddenly materialized before him – the pretty face of Sargam. Just the thought of Sargam's company acted as an instant invigorant, springing him to life once again. If there was one person he truly wanted to share his accomplishments and a lot more with, it was her.

Abhigyan Kukreti

Abhigyan, a third generation migrant to Delhi, was a wanderer at heart. Only, this realization had dawned upon him much later in life, when his ignorance of his own character had already inflicted considerable damage on his otherwise peaceful life.

Coming from a family of academics – a public servant father and a lecturer mother – he had an obligatory association with books from an early age. Pepped up and sometimes prodded by his parents, he had readily substituted books for most of his other boyish needs – video games, television and even friends. So, while he had succeeded in bringing a smile to his parents' face each time they received his report card, his social skills had taken a mauling in the process. Other kids from school and even his neighbourhood considered him a bore. When they teased or bullied him, Abhigyan could rarely come up with a befitting retort, meekly resigning to becoming the butt of their jokes.

It was a pitiable state indeed, but Abhigyan rarely pitied himself. He derived his consolation from the knowledge he was accumulating, the marks he scored and the overwhelming satisfaction it brought to his parents. The other kids, in his mind, were incapable of matching his achievements and hence took to venting their frustrations by mocking him. He was superior to them in several ways and it was them he pitied instead.

As the years went by, the rift between Abhigyan and his peers only widened. Unsuspectingly, an unfamiliar variable had also crept into the equation – gender classification. Girls had always been around him, but all of a sudden they had started sounding, looking and behaving differently than the boys. And bizarrely, their presence proved even more foreboding for Abhigyan than that of the boys. He found himself fidgeting and shifting his gaze nervously whenever a girl initiated dialogue with him, a rare occurrence anyway. Even if it was as simple a thing as seeking directions, when it came to girls, Abhigyan could hardly ever progress beyond a mutter.

He was nevertheless curious about the breed. They looked alluring, at least most of them, and in private he would often fantasize about metamorphosing into a man they couldn't stop drooling over. Some of the guys he had grown up with had a way with girls. He had seen them make small talk, crack jokes, laugh, hug and even take one or the other girl out for a movie – a date, they would call it. He would sulk in private, but not find it within him to even attempt striking a conversation with someone of the opposite sex. This vexation had acquired the form of a deep-rooted abhorrence over time and Abhigyan had come to hate the entire female race, his mother serving as the only exception.

It was when he, aided by his ever-loyal books, managed to secure admission in a reputed medical college that Abhigyan, the loner, decided it was time for him to transform. To the best of his knowledge, none of those who went to school with him were to attend the same college. This implied that he could conveniently relinquish the baggage of his past and start afresh. He could now shamelessly ape the things that made some guys more popular than the others – their mannerisms, their clothes, their style – and who knew, he might even be able to 'date' a girl or two.

Abhigyan gave the makeover his best shot, but the bubble didn't take long before bursting. Firstly, it wasn't easy to instantaneously give up the personality he had acquired over the past several years of his life. Each attempt he made to talk to a girl was like trial by fire for him and he never found himself at ease in their company. He would have to plan his dialogues, rehearse them in his mind, and if by some stroke of misfortune the conversation began heading towards uncharted frontiers, his tongue would fail him. The effort it was taking made Abhigyan wonder if it was all actually worth it.

Secondly, the girls here were not as enticing as those he had gone to school with. The gender ratio in the medical college was as it is unfavourable, with an average count of one female per twenty five males, and generally speaking, the girls here were mostly variants of his personality that he was desperately trying to run away from – bothered more about academics than their appearance, unsophisticated and aloof.

Consequently, it was only a matter of time that he gave up on his transformation endeavour and slipped back into the mould of his comfort. Among the few initiatives he had taken as a part of his efforts to change, the one that stuck was his fitness regime. His analysis from the past that fitter guys had better chances of striking it with girls had prompted him to sign up for the college gym. However, once the initial muscular resistance to the strain had waned, he had begun enjoying the rhythm of the treadmill and the cross trainer. So, even as the futility of his chase had dawned upon him, he had persisted with his visits to the gym with no ulterior motives to guide him this time around.

He had always been academically inclined, thus, it came as no surprise when Abhigyan topped his class in the first semester examinations. The parameters of success in medical college were very different from where he had come from, and this feat – one that was a constant cause for his ridicule back at school – made him promptly soar up the popularity charts here. He became a sought after commodity overnight as his colleagues vied to become a part of his group for group-study and projects, ensuring that Abhigyan was always surrounded by people. He wasn't complaining about the adulation and attention that had involuntarily come his way.

It was perhaps this surge in his popularity that gave him his first taste of physical proximity with a girl. It was sometime after the first semester results that he was idling away at the tea-stall outside the college gate with some of the boys. It was way past 1.00 a.m. and they, having just completed an assignment which was due for submission the next morning, had decided to take a quick break before retiring to their hostel. The tea-stall, like on most nights, was buzzing with activity as several groups of students happily chatted away while sipping on the sugary, hot beverage.

The tea-stall was like a lifeline for the campus. It not only offered the fraught students their daily dose of caffeine, but also doubled up as a recreational hub for those desirous of a recess between their night-time readings. All through the night, hordes of students congregated at the stall, chitchatting and engaging in frivolous banter, soaking in the vibrancy to see them through what remained of the night.

Abhigyan and the two others accompanying him were still in their first year, and hence had to tread cautiously when it came to frolic, for the fear of attracting undue attention of their seniors. Seniors in the medical college were a class of people to be revered as well as feared, forcibly sometimes, and staying away from their gaze was the most obvious thing for newbies to do.

So, at a distance from the other more homogeneous groups, the three sat down and ordered their tea. Unlike the guffawing and loud banters emanating from the other groups, their conversation was largely subdued, alternating between matters relating to the assignment they had just completed and trivialities like cinema and sports. It was then that Abhigyan saw her for the first time. She was sitting among a bunch of seniors, looking fixedly at him – a little too brazenly as far as he was concerned. Their eyes met briefly and he was quick to avert his gaze for the fear of the obvious. But strangely, in that brief moment she had neither attempted to look away and nor extended a courteous smile of acknowledgment. It was as if she were appraising a frog to dissect in the laboratory.

Abhigyan looked at his companions. They were both busy debating over the suspect bowling action of a newly inducted Sri Lankan cricketer (at 2.00 in the morning, imagine!) and he was glad that they hadn't been privy to the brief optical exchange that had just transpired. From the corner of his eye he glanced at the group. There were five of them, two girls and three boys, their seniors clearly, but Abhigyan did not know any of them. The girl, a bespectacled, average-looking dame with wheatish complexion and unkempt but rather dense hair, was still eyeing him vehemently. He had to turn away rather quickly to avoid catching her gaze once again.

He had himself gulped down his tea in quick time and was glad when the other two, between their highly animated discussion, managed to empty their glasses as well. The three leisurely strolled back to the campus, stopping only when the entrance to the first hostel block, where Abhigyan's two companions shared a room, came into sight. As luck would have it, he still had two blocks to pass and a climb of three flights of stairs before reaching his room.

'Hey you,' he heard someone call out as he was crossing the gravel path between the second and the third block. Startled, he turned around, only to find the girl from the tea-stall scampering towards him. She was alone, her mates nowhere in sight.

'You are Abhigyan, right? The same guy who has topped in the first semester?' she quizzed as soon as she had caught up with him. She was short, standing almost half a foot lower than him, but voluptuously built. She was wearing a grey collared t-shirt with black slacks, lending her a casual yet in-control look.

'Yes,' Abhigyan uttered, unsure of what to expect.

'Well, hi, I am Neeta… third year,' she said, jutting her hand forward. Her hand, as Abhigyan shook it, was firm and had a coarse texture. It was as if he had been holding another man's hand rather than a woman's.

'I heard someone talk about you the other day and since then I have been hoping to speak to you. You see, one of my seniors had given me a set of anatomy and physiology notes for the second semester curriculum. These notes cover the entire syllabus in barely a few hundred pages and are far easier to comprehend than most of the prescribed textbooks. They helped me pass my second semester with flying colours,' she began, her eyes intently focused on Abhigyan's puzzled face.

'I thought I had lost them until a few days back, when I was cleaning my room, they materialized out of nowhere. I really value these notes and hence didn't want to give them out to just about anybody. So, when I heard about you I knew that with you they would be in the right hands. Would you want to have them?'

Abhigyan didn't know what to say. Obviously, she hadn't followed him all the way from the tea-stall in the middle of the night driven by her magnanimity. The notes, if they indeed existed, would of course come in handy, but there had to be something else on Neeta's mind.

'Come with me, I will give you the notes,' sensing his hesitation, she directed, walking past him. Abhigyan, at a loss of wit, meekly followed. Ahead of him he could see her curvaceous posterior, pressing against the tight synthetic fabric of the slacks, moving with a swagger that was enough to set his innards on fire.

Like a zombie he followed her down the winding path, into the red-brick block of the girls hostel, up the flights of stairs – he had no clue how many – to her room. Neeta pulled a switch to bring the lamp on her study table to life. It was a cosy room, like the single rooms of seniors in his hostel, but better maintained. There were no clothes strewn around on the bed or elsewhere, the walls were adorned with posters – tasteful black-and-white landscapes, but for the lone Sylvester Stallone centrefold behind the wooden door.

'Relax, sit down. I will be back in a jiffy,' she said, excavating a towel from one of the wooden drawers and stepping out of the room. Abhigyan gently lowered himself on the bed, weary, as if it were made of thorns. He urgently needed to divert his attention away from where it was shamelessly affixed if he were to avoid shaming himself. So, pressing his thighs hard together, he got down to studying the floral patterns on the pink-white bed sheet.

She returned in little time, as promised. Only, the clothes she had been wearing were now bundled up beneath her arms and the towel wrapped around her body, fastened around the chest and dangling till her thighs. Strands of her now wet hair were clinging to her body, partly shielding her sinuous cleavage from his view. As she stepped forward, the towel parting slightly, the sight forced an inaudible gasp out of him. She smelled sweet – a mix of lavender and vanilla – and no matter how hard he tried, he could not take his eyes off her.

Without a word, she stepped towards him and in one swift motion lifted her right leg to place her knee somewhere between his chest and abdomen. Pushing him gently, she crawled atop him, losing the towel along the way. Abhigyan had shut his eyes involuntarily and as his hands reached out for her, he felt his fingers rest on her dewy yet warm flesh. She was stark naked, a realization that set a volcano erupting deep within him.

What followed was a night of unbridled and raw passion, nothing like anything Abhigyan had ever experienced. Neeta Nair, a girl from the southern shores of the country, as he later learnt, had taken him for an intergalactic jaunt and back in that little time. She had been completely in control, guiding and urging him to experience the ultimate heights of passion, and he neither had a reason, nor the inclination to record a protest.

'You were good. We must get together more often,' were her parting words as he emerged from her room in the wee hours of the morning. The notes she had meant to give him were never spoken of thereafter.

The thrilling journey he had embarked upon that night continued for several months, till she began her house surgeonship – a mandatory 12-month internship for her MBBS degree that kept her in one or the other hospital ward on most nights. Perhaps the excitement in their relationship had been waning too and Abhigyan was only glad to allow it to slip into oblivion. It had been a relationship of convenience – one meant to quench bodily hunger and not the emotional thirst of the partakers – but it had played a significant role in shaping the Abhigyan of today. Neeta had made him taste blood, and it was only a matter of time before he embarked on a hunt to satiate his cravings.

He was party to several other flings before graduating from the medical college with a Doctor of Medicine (MD) degree, but none capable of holding his attention for long. Abhigyan was a changed man now. He relished the company of girls, especially the titillating perks that came along, but once he returned home, he was compelled to put his longings to rest. He had changed, but his parents had not, and neither had their expectations from him. To them he was still the little boy who, with his academic exultations, was en route to earning accolades and glory for the family. Abhigyan, on his part, didn't have the heart to shatter their hopes. He was constrained, but his familiarity with these controls made him view them as definitive rather than a thing to be challenged or negotiated.

He started his career as a junior doctor with a private nursing home, bifurcating his time between caring for his ailing patients and elderly parents. It was around this time, upon his parents' insistence, that Abhigyan gave his consent for marriage.

The girl in question, Shikha, was an MBA by qualification and a banker by profession. Since it was an arranged set-up, the only parameter Abhigyan had to judge her on was her looks. His parents had already done hygiene investigations into her family background, combined prophecies of their stars and the likes. And her petite frame, dreamy eyes, pinkish-cream complexion and most notably, as far as Abhigyan was concerned, her shapely figure, left him with little reason to decline the proposed alliance.

The marriage was solemnized amid much fanfare and was followed by a honeymoon trip to Langkawi – a picturesque island off the Malaysian mainland. To Shikha, this was the culmination of a dream she had been cultivating ever since she had grown up enough to participate in the doll-weddings the girls in her neighbourhood would organize. It was a special phase, a phase marking her transition to womanhood, and she meant to treasure every moment, every speck that made it. Although for Abhigyan it was more about exploring the legitimate proximity to another pretty girl that marriage accorded, it proved every bit the exhilarating experience that honeymoons are meant to be.

Following this promising start, their life together continued on its melodious path. They were one big happy family: the doctor – as devoted to his family as his patients, the wife – a demure banker by the day and a hopeless romantic by the night, and the pleased, ageing parents. No telling how far this fantastical set-up would have persisted had it not been for the alternate plans fate had in store for them.

It was a dark monsoon evening, its malleable character open to being moulded as per each heart's desire. To Abhigyan, who had just returned home after a particularly harrowing day, it was the perfect setting for romance and amorous cravings. He had recently started his clinic and was yet to come to terms with the hectic juggling between the two workplaces and the respective set of patients. Tired, when he had finally set off for home, the agreeable weather had infused a sudden spurt of excitement within him. A hot cup of coffee, some crispy pakoras and... well, his mind had suddenly come alive with a tenacious voracity.

'Where is Mummy?' he inquired, sensing the unusual quiet. He, having dumped his work-bag and shoes, was slouched on the couch fiddling with the remote. In the meantime, Shikha, having let him in, was heading for the kitchen.

'They have gone to Brigadier uncle's party, left only a short while back,' she shot back.

'Oh, yes.'

'Water,' she said, approaching him with a tray. 'Shall I also make some tea for you?'

She was still in her office wear – a pair of slender, snug-fitting trousers and a halter-top that did well to accentuate her shapely torso. Especially striking was the thin belt, about a quarter of an inch in width, carelessly wrapped around her waist. This was how he found her most alluring.

'Later,' he said, using the excuse of returning the glass to the tray for holding her hand. In one swift jerk, he pulled her small frame atop him, sending the glass and the tray clinkering.

'Stop it,' she resisted, the tone more than betraying her lack of conviction.

It wasn't an opportunity that the young couple frequently got. Sharing the house with Abhigyan's parents implied that they hardly ever got to express their love for each other outside the closed confines of their bedroom, let alone brazenly make out on the living room couch. Consumed by the thrill of the prohibited, the two attacked each other with fierce passion, shredding each garment from their midst as though it were an undesired blood-sucking leech.

Their tangle would have lasted long, but for the sudden interruption. When the shrilling noise of the telephone ring interrupted them, they were both drenched in sweat and panting.

'Uh…Hullo,' Abhigyan muttered, dragging himself to the incessantly buzzing instrument with sufficient struggle.

'Is this A-13, Defence Colony?'

The voice on the line was gruff yet officious sounding, and there was an ominous urgency about the manner in which the question had been posed.

'Yes,' he confirmed, slightly alarmed.

'There has been an accident and we got your number from the parking sticker on the car,' the man began, Abhigyan's expression changing from shock to disbelief to fear with every word that he heard.

'How are they? Are they hurt?'

As it turned out, the clouds had opened their doors in certain parts of the city, including where Abhigyan's parents were headed. The lashing rains, like a maze of psychedelic sheets had concealed every opaque form within its folds, and it was in this diminished visibility that Abhigyan's father failed to negotiate the divider and drove right into it. It couldn't have been the impact of the collision, for the old man rarely ever permitted the speedometer to breach sixty; perhaps the angle, because of which the car toppled over and landed on its roof.

A couple of patrolling policemen had reached the site and sent the two passengers to a nearby hospital. It was one of them who had called Abhigyan.

When Abhigyan reached the hospital, his mother was still in coma, and his father, albeit conscious, was on the ICU bed with an oxygen mask cupping his mouth. For the next two days, he kept battling his destiny, running from pillar to post and using all his medical acumen and connections to retrieve his parents from the calamitous jaws of death. Towards the end of the second day, without a cue, his mother's condition began to deteriorate and within a matter of hours she had slipped from her comatose state into the zone of no return. It was a painless death, the doctors claimed, but for Abhigyan it was more painful than anything he had ever experienced. His mother had deprived him even of the chance to say goodbye.

The old man, challenged by the double whammy of his injuries and the news of his wife's death, couldn't hold on to the thread of life for much longer either. Three days following his wife's demise, he too eventually succumbed to his injuries. Even as his mother's funeral pyre continued to simmer, Abhigyan had to get down to planning his father's last rites. Shikha stood by him all this while, aggrieved and agitated, but poised enough to stand by her distraught husband like a pillar of strength. Only, she had no way of knowing how this tragic development was to impact her own life over the coming months.

The unexpected tragedy left Abhigyan jolted from within. His parents had been there by his side for as far back as he could remember, whether he had needed them or not. Never ever had he imagined a day when he would have to carry on with life in their absence, and now they were suddenly gone. Forever. Never to return. His mother would never cook his favourite dishes now, and his father would not be around to guide him on matters of finance or investments. The fears he had prevented from breaching even his imagination had suddenly turned real and were mocking his helplessness.

He found his immediate reprieve in work and alcohol. He dreaded returning home, to the same house where his mother had once waited on him. So, when he ran out of patients to keep him at bay, he would hit the bar and let the alcohol take over his senses. Entering the house under the veil of inebriation was any day better than doing so when he was sober. Shikha could only imagine the sting of his agony and so she let Abhigyan chart his own course uninterrupted. The drinking was temporary, she would tell herself, and she had no business interfering with it if it helped alleviate his sufferings.

Only, Abhigyan's dismal state was anything but transitory. One thing led to the other and he soon found himself swimming along a familiar frontier – the pursuit of women. Construing Shikha's non-interference for nonchalance he began to consciously expand the web of his debauchery. His patients, employees of the hospital and women he met at the bar, anyone who was willing was fair game to him. His escapades became so recurrent that an unauthorized guesthouse, run from a private bungalow in East of Kailash, permanently had a room booked under his name.

When he travelled abroad, usually to attend sponsored medical conferences, he would hardly ever show up at the conference venues. Instead he would spend his days and nights locked up with prostitutes in his hotel rooms. In fact in his closer circles it was even believed that in certain Amsterdam brothels, one could get a discount by simply mentioning Dr. Abhigyan Kukreti's name.

His decline was steep and by the time Shikha woke up to the need for her interference, the matter was already beyond redemption. Abhigyan was remorseless and brazen about his depravity, not even bothering about a smokescreen to shield his doings. If ever Shikha happened to enquire about his whereabouts, he would simply ignore the question. Lipstick marks on his collars, unannounced night-outs and hushed telephonic conversations at strange hours had become a norm in the house and no one, not even his wife, had the right to question him. If Shikha did voice her concerns, she would fare no better than if she were attempting to strike conversation with one of the living room walls.

The situation was extremely frustrating for her. There was no one that she could share her predicament with and allowing the issues to weigh down on her mind had begun to impact her performance at work as well. The loop was never-ending, as suddenly there was no one left at home for her to discuss her workplace concerns with either. But despite the impediments, she held on to some invisible ray of hope for months, wishing that the man she was sharing the house with would once again turn into her loving husband and she would be reinstated on the path to realizing her many dreams alongside him.

When the thread of her patience eventually snapped, she did what any self-respecting woman in her place would have done, and perhaps much earlier – filed for divorce. She moved out of the house, to the one she had come from, and after the mandatory six-months of separation lapsed, the family court granted divorce by mutual consent to Dr. Abhigyan Kukreti and Shikha Aggarwal.

Nothing much changed in Abhigyan's life with Shikha's departure, not immediately at least. He remained absorbed in his vices, indifferent to all else surrounding him.

It was much later and very gradually that loneliness began to show up in his life in the form of occasional but agonizing pangs. After the departure of his parents, Abhigyan had buried himself in sinfulness to plug the void they had left behind. But Shikha had been there, discreetly persevering in the background. He did not realize then, but her presence, like a pot of gold buried somewhere in one's backyard, had been a latent source of comfort and security. And now, given her absence, he had suddenly become meek, vulnerable and isolated. He of course could not go back to her now, after the treatment he had ruthlessly meted out to her, but he needed to find another way to plug this glaring crevice in the structure of his existence. And thus began Abhigyan's search for a second wife.

It wasn't that he was deprived of women in his life, there were many he could summon by way of a simple phone call, and that he did when his carnal instincts took over, but none of them were 'marriage material'. The motley bunch was bound by the selfishness of their motives behind their presence in his life – lust, passion and occasionally money. None of them loved him for what he was, and of course he didn't much care about them either.

He created his profile on several matchmaking sites, chatted up with potential brides, but only to realize that he, despite his remarkable material qualifications wasn't exactly hot property in the marital market anymore. The tag of being a divorcee acted as an impregnable filter when it came to most profiles he found interesting. And the ones who reciprocated were usually those looking to settle for a compromise to cover their own deficiencies – mediocre looks, excessive weight, or like him, history of a prior marriage.

In the absence of his parents, who had found him one perfect bride and could possibly have even found another, Abhigyan's search was just about dragging along. At times its unpromising nature made him want to abandon his pursuit entirely, but the fear of an isolated and lonely senectitude kept him going. He was aware that none of his present-day companions would last through his declining years and the thought of growing old without a hand to hold or a shoulder to rest his head on made him cringe.

It was in this discouraging phase of his quest that he met Lalkrishna, and through him, Sargam. Instantly he knew that his search was on the verge of completion. He had met many potential brides till then, but Sargam was the only one to have evoked memories of Shikha and the healthier times from his past. It wasn't right, Abhigyan knew, to compare anyone else with Shikha, but this had inadvertently become a measure his subconscious relied upon to judge the prospective girls he met. And thus, when he first set his eyes on her – poised, confident and yet confined, just like Shikha had once been – a surge of hope shot through him like a bullet.

Sargam had everything he wished for in his partner – the exuberance of youth, eyes that bespoke affection, tenderness and unfulfilled dreams, and a body that elicited interest and a curious yearning. Her sight evoked a strange array of emotions within him – a paternalistic need to cuddle and protect her, a childish want to be pampered by her, and a passionate urge to become one with her. In her he could see the answer to his questions and the culmination of his pursuit.

Another detail that he noticed during his maiden meeting with Sargam was her utter disinterest in him. It was evident that she was there not to evaluate a conjugal union, but to merely make good her father's word. The realization, albeit slightly distressing, was perfectly comprehendible as Sargam would have easily found a match more suitable than Abhigyan. In light of this, he even managed to convince himself that Sargam was a case of the proverbial sour grapes and that he should forget her and move on.

His resolve, however, lasted for barely a few hours following their meeting. Sargam's thoughts simply refused to let go of him, no matter how hard he tried. Her smile, her pretty face, her voice, the humiliation of her rejection, the texture of her skin, her lusciously pouted lips and her inviting curves kept rummaging through his mind at will, leaving him panting and craving for her. In less than 24 hours, it was clear to him that he couldn't just forget Sargam and move on. He had to do something, anything, to make her his own.

Lalkrishna, Sargam's father, was a man of the world, and it wasn't hidden from Abhigyan that the old man was smitten by his stature and financial standing. Lalkrishna's desire to get his daughter married to an affluent man was the only thing going in the doctor's favour and he decided to use this to his advantage.

He began by way of intermittent courtesy calls to Lalkrishna, surreptitiously selling his candidature as their prospective son-in-law, if ever any selling was needed. Once he was certain of having aligned her father, he began exploiting this influence to be able to meet Sargam. And he succeeded.

His ploy was simple: he somehow needed to impress her enough and lead her to his bed. He knew such virtuous girls well.

Once he was able to penetrate the veil of her morality, she would become his. The very shield of scruples that his advances were bouncing back from would then prevent her from ever dreaming about another man. And it was to this end that he had been laboriously working towards for the past several weeks.

To his credit, he had been meeting her on a fairly regular basis now, although still with Lalkrishna's intervention. In fact even the last evening he had met her at a food-court in one of the South Delhi Malls, a venue he despised for its absence of privacy, but for Sargam's insistence. He had persisted with his attempts to invite her home, but she had excused herself on account of a headache, a long day at work perhaps. Another day then, he had told himself, watching her sputter away in an auto rickshaw.

His fascination with Sargam was now acquiring near obsessive proportions. Barely a few hours after seeing her off, as he poured himself a drink within the cosy confines of his living room, her thoughts came back to haunt him. It had become almost ritualistic now – imagining her presence, talking out aloud to her and envisioning the lifeless pillow he clutched to sleep to be Sargam. The social encounters were no longer proving enough. He needed her by his side at all times, urgently and desperately.

The next morning, today, began with its usual frenzy for Dr. Abhigyan Kukreti. All through the day his clinic was thronged by patients, leaving little space for his thoughts to meander elsewhere. Late in the evening, much later than usual, when he had attended to the last of his patients, he was filled with an inexplicable feeling of contentment. A brief glance at the day's billing summary was enough to confirm that it had indeed been a day of brisk business. He had grossed his highest ever collection as a private medical practitioner today – a staggering sum of over two lakh fifty thousand rupees. His father would have been particularly proud of his feat.

He slumped on his chair, fighting a strong urge to celebrate the day's achievement. There was no one he could think of inviting to join him at such a late hour. And then, on a sudden impulse, he reached out for the phone on his desk and dialled Lalkrishna's number. After the customary greetings, he asked for Sargam. Obviously, he couldn't meet her right then, but at least he could share his jubilation with her telephonically. After all, wasn't companionship all about sharing these little moments? She might not regard him as her partner just as yet, but who knew, these little cues might make all the difference.

'She usually returns home much earlier, but today she is working late,' Lalkrishna replied apologetically.

His immediate reaction was one of disappointment. He contemplated reaching her on her mobile, but changed his mind before his fingers could play on the dial. Although he had her number for a while now, he had never called her directly but for the purpose of coordination during their prearranged meetings. And if she was still at work, it wasn't a particularly wise time to press the pedal any further.

It was later, as he was sipping his drink all by himself that the thought occurred to him. Was she indeed in her office at this hour? Wasn't this one of the surest excuses to feed her parents if she was engaging in something she didn't want them to know about? Was it possible that she was seeing someone and was in her lover's arms that very instant? Why not! It was certainly plausible, probable in fact. She was young and good-looking, why couldn't she be dating someone?

Each question, as it erupted within his head, pumped him with a fresh gush of rage. He was jealous, a feeling he was neither familiar, nor comfortable with. The fact that he had no way of quashing his suspicions was only fuelling his anger further. The only thing he could do then was to drink away the disturbing thought, and that he did with consummate fervor, losing count of the number of drinks he guzzled. It was only when the empty bottle stared back at him from the table that he eventually pulled himself up from the sofa. His mind was numb now, painless and insulated, and he was ready to hit the bed.

29th December

Sharib Sheikh

Sharib woke up with a start, a calculating ferocity emerging in his eyes, as he cursed himself for having fallen asleep. He could hear voices within his head: accusatory ones – 'you have stolen the money, give it back', and pleading ones – 'please return the money, it belongs to my office'. Last night, when he had conjured these scenes, the voices had a face too – Sargam's face – and he was glad that only the audio remained now. The audio-visual combination was quite distressing as he had already experienced.

He looked around. Afzal, his roommate was sprawled on the nearby mattress, an incessant gurgle emanating from somewhere between his nose and his throat. He must have returned late in the night, sometime after Sharib had lost his battle with sleep.

The excruciating pain of being accused of theft by the very girl he was so madly in love with was still lingering, ferociously stabbing his innards every once in a while. The moment he thought about the pain, his mind darted back to the solution he had come up with to alleviate it. It was the reprieve of having come up with this plan to rescue himself from the agonizing quandary that had lolled him to sleep, he recalled. Instantly the conflicting arguments from last night, those he had presumed to have settled once and for all, began to once again sprout within his head.

Was this the right thing to do? A girl who remained oblivious to his feelings for her, did she deserve such a sacrifice? Not meaning to lose his focus, he brushed aside these thoughts, deliberately draining them with the counter arguments that had originally helped him make up his mind.

'True test of love is not when it shows up in a perfectly penned-down plot, but when all odds are stacked against it. Sargam might not love him, not just as yet at least, but that shouldn't form the basis for his actions. If he was certain of his love for her, shouldn't he be behaving just as he would if his affection was acknowledged and reciprocated? She might not have said it in as many words, but she was clearly in a jam. Losing money that belonged to her employers could have severe implications; she might even end up losing her job. And who knew what circumstances at the personal front had made her take up a job in the first place. If he, a man who claimed to be in love with her, was not to come to her rescue, who would? Moreover, wasn't this the only way for him to redeem himself?' Having successfully washed down his reservations under the shower of well-meditated urgings, Sharib pulled himself up from the bed. What he intended to do did not allow for any form of reproach in his heart, only the knowledge that he was doing so for the sake of his love.

He stepped out of the room, on to the terrace and splashed a handful of water from the plastic bucket to his face. It was pretty early in the day, at least a couple of hours too early for the business he had in mind. But sitting and waiting for time to lapse wasn't a particularly bright idea as far as Sharib was concerned. There was every chance that the resistance within him would once again rear its head, making the task ahead much more challenging. Thus, pulling his shirt from the nail on the wall, he emerged from his dwelling, and jerking the auto rickshaw to life, set out on the desolate early morning Delhi streets.

He traced the roads through Ashram to South Extension, stopping in-between for a cup of tea at a roadside stall, but did not come across a single passenger. It was a Sunday and the city was taking its time to emerge from its slumber.

At around 9.30, he stopped the auto outside Seth ji's house, ambled across to the doorsill and pressed the call bell. In a few minutes he was ushered inside by the domestic help, into the large living room that doubled up as an office. Sharib had been here before, when he had first set out to find his footing in the city and several times thereafter. The room hadn't changed much. It was still the image of tasteless opulence that Sharib remembered it to be, with assorted adornments – expensive but garish – lining the corners and the walls. An incense stick was simmering somewhere, perhaps on the pedestal where large three-dimensional paintings of several deities, embellished with golden metalwork, were placed. Sharib stood, inhaling the aromatic fumes, waiting for the master of the house to emerge. There were sofas and chairs in the room, but from prior experience Sharib knew that these were not meant for drivers who drove Sethi ji's autos. And despite having bought a vehicle of his own now, Sharib, in the eyes of the domestic help, had not come up to a level where he needed to be offered a seat.

'Oh… Sharib! What a pleasant surprise! Long time, how have you been?' Seth ji's rotund frame emerged from the anteroom and greeted him in his usual jovial manner. 'Tell me, what is it?'

He puffed under the strain of depositing his bulk on the sofa. He refrained from offering Sharib a seat either.

'I had tried calling your number last evening, but couldn't get through. In fact, I wanted to see you about what you had said a couple of months back,' Sharib began, reminding the Seth of their brief exchange from the evening he had accompanied Afzal to return Seth ji's auto after his shift had ended. The duo had planned to go to Jama Masjid for offering prayers that evening and Sharib had offered to drive them in his auto once Afzal had returned the rented one to its owner. Then too Seth ji had greeted Sharib enthusiastically, and glancing at his well-kept vehicle, said, 'It is good to see that you are making quick progress, and that's a nice pair of wheels you've got. How much did you pay for it?'

Sharib, flushed at the compliment, had muttered the amount he had purchased the second-hand vehicle for. Of course, he had spent a considerable sum in bringing the vehicle up to how it looked then, but he refrained from mentioning it to avoid complicating his reply.

'Wow, that's quite a bargain. If ever you are looking to sell it off, let me know. I will be happy to match what you've paid for it,' the Seth had added.

'About?' Seth ji replied, quizzically pulling his brows together. He clearly did not recall the conversation.

'About my auto… You had said that you would be interested in buying it if ever I was selling. I am in dire need of some money and so I was looking to sell the vehicle.'

Seth ji mulled over the proposition with a soft hum. 'How much are you expecting for it?' he said after a brief pause.

'I had bought it for a lakh and twenty thousand rupees. And I will be happy to let you have it for as much.'

'What? You know that the price of vehicles depreciates with each passing day, don't you? And how many months have you driven it since you paid that kind of money for it?' Seth ji's tone was laden with incredulity, and this, to Sharib, was somewhat unsettling. For him a lot depended on this transaction going through and the thought that the Seth might retract his words had not even occurred to him till then.

'But I have spent over fifteen thousand rupees in overhauling the vehicle, an amount I am not even looking to recover. Moreover, you had said that you will match the price I had paid to purchase it,' Sharib reasoned.

'I might have said so, but that was then. Today is a different day altogether. Wait, let me inspect the vehicle and see what best I can offer for it,' he said, dismissing Sharib's reasoning to engage in the arduous task of lifting himself from the sofa.

'Ninety thousand, not a paisa more,' he said after spending a good ten minutes in scanning the length and breadth of the auto rickshaw. 'Don't just take my word for it, go and try your luck in the market too. You will be fortunate to find someone willing to pay even close to what I have offered.'

Sharib did not have the luxury of time to seek a better bargain elsewhere, and he suspected that this fact wasn't hidden from Seth ji either. Therefore, after slight bit of haggling, the deal was wrapped for a consideration of ninety-five thousand rupees.

Sharib had brought the vehicle's ownership documents with him – the registration certificate, permit and insurance papers, all in the name of the previous owner, and a form for the transfer of ownership, duly signed by the previous owner as well. This was standard practice when it came to buying or selling auto rickshaws and Sharib hadn't bothered to get the vehicle transferred to his name.

Seth ji, after keenly inspecting the papers, nodded his approval, and asking Sharib to grab a seat, vanished inside the house.

He emerged a little later, holding a wad of notes, all thousands. The world of auto rickshaws and most of the commerce therein transpired well beneath the radar of account books and tax authorities. By implication, therefore, the preferred mode for all monetary dealings was cash. It was cash that Sharib had used to pay for the vehicle and it was cash he was now carrying back in lieu of it, only a tad short of his urgent and pressing need.

Instead of hailing a bus or an auto, he opted to walk back home. An isolated stroll felt much safer, given the discernible outline of the bundle which he had deposited in his trouser pocket. Plus, he needed the solitude to get his bearings straight. It was a long walk, but the weather was agreeable and he would get the own-time he needed to come to terms with the drastic step he had just taken. Its purpose notwithstanding, giving up his life's earnings, his only symbol of hope, was an act facing stiff resistance from a part of him, the rational side perhaps.

And now, as he neared the point of no return, the point where he would have made his offering to his love, rendering futile any subsequent changes of heart, the opposition within him was making a last ditch effort to have its say. He had as much time as his walk lasted to resolve this inner conflict. Once home, and if Afzal happened to be around, he would have to get on with it immediately, without the luxury of any time to deliberate further. Any idling about beyond the perfunctory freshening up and perhaps a quick change of clothes was bound to attract Afzal's curiosity. And the last thing Sharib wanted to deal with then was an external ally for his mind's pragmatic arguments against his own decision. There was no way for Afzal to comprehend his actions, let alone agree with them.

Sargam Joshi

For Sargam, the night had been a vague outline connecting her many moments of consciousness. Interspersed within were blank spaces induced by irrepressible spells of sleep or the hysteria of her frenzied thoughts. So, while just a minute ago she had been sodden in darkness – of the night as well as the melancholy of her own spirit – the very next instant she was bathed in the steely gray of dawn, all with the orchestra of chirping fowls and the continuous drone of a rising city.

It had been a laborious night, but that was past now. A new dawn was breaking, the day that separated her from her destiny was here and she needed to make it count, anyhow, somehow. Thankfully it was Sunday and she wasn't expected to be up early. So she opted in favour of lolling around in her room for a while. It wasn't that she had much thinking left to do, she had done enough of it through the night, but the action plan she had charted out for herself needed all the courage and resolve she could muster. She was thus thinking about myriad things, affirmative ones which had the slightest chance of infusing optimism and hope.

It was well past nine when she eventually emerged from the room. 'Have you had your tea? I am making some,' her mother yelled from the kitchen. Her father, expectedly, was nowhere to be seen. There was still some time before Lalkrishna's lethargic day would officially begin.

'No, I have some work…Need to rush,' she shouted back, deriving a flash of satisfaction at being the object of her mother's concern.

In less than twenty minutes Sargam was stepping inside the Srinivaspuri Police Station, albeit a little reluctantly. Till now her only visibility of a police station's interiors had been through films and television, and as she braced herself to actually enter one, she couldn't help but feel intimidated and confused. The large hall that greeted her was swarming with people even at that early hour, mostly men – a blend of law-enforcers and law-breakers, she mused – adding to her unease. Briefly surveying the surroundings, she stepped towards a relatively uncrowded counter where a bespectacled policeman, his nose buried inside a thick register, was seated.

'Sir...I need to file a complaint,' she hesitantly muttered. The man took his time wrenching his eyes from the log, pushing his spectacles with a practiced movement of his forefinger to meet her gaze. He had a look of incredulity in his eyes, as though she had just descended from a different planet. After an unnerving, drawn-out pause, he curtly replied, 'There, that's the complaints desk. Sit over there and you will be summoned when your turn comes.' Sargam, without bothering to thank him, turned on her heels and made for the most crowded section of the room. The bench she had been directed to was already crammed with four men and a boy strangely squeezing their derrieres to claim it, leaving her with no option but to stand and await her turn.

It was after much priming that she had been able to shed her inhibitions and drag herself to the police station. She knew that this was the right and perhaps the only thing left for her to do, and yet the anxiety within her was once again welling up.

She had spent a considerable part of the night contemplating it, playing and replaying her telephonic conversation with the auto-wallah in her head. There was little doubt that she had done the best she could do under the circumstances, but the question was whether that was going to prove enough. Was he likely to succumb to her threat and meekly return the money? Despite her optimism, the answer she got to this question was in the negative. These guys (auto drivers) were hardened men, used to facing severities more profound than a mere verbal threat from a girl. Her naivety had probably given him reason for a hearty laugh, nothing more.

If she were to give herself any real shot at getting the money back, she needed to substantiate her words with actions, and the only way she could think of doing it was by lodging a police complaint. And if she had to approach the authorities, she needed to do so urgently, without wasting any more time. They were bound to question the timing of her complaint and an inexplicable delay was certain to cast aspersions on her credibility. Moreover, what if the auto-wallah were to elope by then? Or, worse still, he could end up spending a significant part of the money he had stolen from her.

'Madam, please come,' she was wrenched out of her reverie by the sudden summon. At least the policeman at the Complaints Desk was vigilant enough to attend to complainants on a first come, first served basis, she mused.

'Please have a seat,' he proffered upon her approach. He was a chubby looking man with bags of flesh dangling on the sides of his chin in a manner that reminded her of a certain breed of dogs. Everything from his movements to the tone of his voice spoke of lassitude and inefficiencies, but for his eyes. His eyes, dark and twinkling, had an alertness that was unsettling and at the same time reassuring to Sargam. He kept appraising her words, silently, as she narrated the entire event, from the time she had left her office with the envelope to her telephonic conversation with Sharib.

'Are you sure that the auto driver stole your money? I mean, it's a long shot that he knew exactly what to look for in your purse in the little time he had. The possibility that the envelope was never inside the purse can't be ruled out,' he said after listening to her account.

'Meaning?' Sargam retorted.

'I mean, you could have forgotten it in the office, or dropped it somewhere…'

'No, I am certain that the envelope was in my purse. I vividly remember having put it there,' she curtly replied. The line of the policeman's questioning was distressing. She was the victim here, and instead of being handed out sympathy and reassurances, she was being interrogated as though she had been the one to commit a crime. The only way she could register her displeasure was through the manner of her replies and she did so by keeping them curt and to the point.

The policeman, once his repertoire of nagging questions had exhausted, penned down her complain in a handwriting that could qualify for Mandarin as much as it could for Hindi. He did ask her for Sharib's description and his phone number, but when Sargam emerged from the police station, her barrel of optimism had drained just that wee bit more. Her secret hope that someone at the station would wave a wand and her lost envelope would magically reappear was certainly not going to play out in reality. If the man to have registered her complaint and the interest he had shown in the case were anything to go by, she would perhaps have been better off visiting a mystic to seek his help instead.

She did have a contingency plan, but Sargam had been desperately hoping that she would be spared its deployment. However, as she hailed an auto to take her home, the gloomy realization that she was left with no other choice dawned upon her. She was aware that the more she deliberated over it, the more resistance she would face from within, and so, pulling out her mobile phone from the handbag, she unsteadily dialled a number.

'Hi, how are you?' she said, cupping her mouth to insulate her words from the din of the running auto.

'Hey, now that's what I call a pleasant surprise! I have been fine. In fact only yesterday evening I was thinking about you. I had even called up your residence number, but you were not back from work by then. How are things with you?' Abhigyan's voice, reeking with excitement, greeted her.

'I am doing fine. Thank you. I had actually called to seek your help over something, but I am not sure how you will react to it...,' she said, allowing her hesitant words to tail. Her ploy wasn't new. In fact women the world over have been consciously or subconsciously using it to have their way with men for eternity. And there was no reason for Abhigyan to skip the bait and not come to the rescue of the damsel in distress, especially given his undying fascination for Sargam.

After he had prompted her a few times, she narrated the happenings of the previous evening to him. 'I have to anyhow return the money to my office by tomorrow, and I was wondering if you would be in a position to lend it to me. I will return it to you over the next few months,' she added.

'Of course you can have the money. And please don't embarrass me by calling it a loan. Whatever belongs to me is yours too, and you can choose to use it as you please.'

'No, I insist. I will only take the money if you promise to take it back later. Don't call it a loan if you despise the word so much, but I will only take it if it is on returnable basis,' she persisted.

'Well, you can make up for it by joining me for a drink this evening. What do you say?'

The negotiations continued for a little while longer, but its conclusion was foregone and known to both concerned parties. Abhigyan was Sargam's last hope of redemption, and as for the money, she needed it at any cost. Abhigyan on the other hand was only too happy to part with whatever sum of money as long as it earned him Sargam's proximity. His focus was clear and he made no bones about it.

The trouble was that his motives were not entirely hidden from Sargam, and to her this was sacrilege. The fact that Abhigyan had been using his proximity with her father to further his own cause didn't help matters either. It was this abhorrence that had made her cringe when sometime during the dark night the thought of borrowing money from Abhigyan had first occurred to her. She had tried to brush it aside, but the ease with which it promised to relieve her of her troubles made it stick. There was little doubt that Abhigyan would give her the money if she ever asked for it, and there was even lesser doubt that he would try and exploit the situation to his advantage.

The mildest word she found in her dictionary to describe such a step was opportunism, but then there was a part of her that was desperate to resolve the issue at hand, no matter what the consequences. The pragmatic side, she liked to believe. 'What will he do? Ask her to join him for dinner at best. He would obviously not try and force himself upon her. If she played her cards right, she could very easily come out of it unscathed. And of course, she would return the money as soon as she was in a position to,' the practical side of her had argued convincingly. Thereafter Sargam had shut out all her thoughts concerning the matter, hoping that a solution would find itself and prevent her from exercising this option. That was till she emerged from the police station, hopeless and distraught.

'Fine then, I will see you at my clinic in the afternoon. From there we will head someplace quiet for a peaceful drink,' Abhigyan summarized the agreed plan once the deal was clinched. For Sargam it had been a battle between her virtues and the urgent need to prevent her life – her career and her aspirations – from collapsing around her. The conversation with Abhigyan had left a lump in her stomach, like she had swallowed a ball of lead. It was weighty and caustic, biting through her innards and making her want to recoil. But then there was the reprieve of another burden being lifted from her shoulders – a burden that had been perilously crushing her since the preceding evening – and she opted to relish this moment of joy, artfully shutting her mind to the agonizing protuberance within her belly.

Abhigyan Kukreti

Abhigyan woke up early, as he usually did when he had been drinking irrepressibly the previous evening. He tried opening his eyes, but his lids felt heavy and the throbbing between his temples made him grimace. His mouth felt stale, and his breath, he was certain, could put any self-respecting skunk to shame. Driven by an urgent need to empty his bladder, he pulled himself up somehow, and clutching the back of his head with one hand, made for the bathroom.

Fifteen minutes later he was slumped on the couch in the drawing room, clutching a cup of black coffee. He had never been much of a cook and the terrible tasting coffee stood testimony to it. It didn't matter much to Abhigyan though. He was more interested in the medicinal value the brew held for him. And indeed, only a few sips of the drink and he could already feel the difference.

It was a Sunday morning and if he were to have his way, Abhigyan wouldn't even have emerged from the bed just as yet. Unless there was some urgent matter to attend, he kept his clinic shut on Sundays, preferring instead to spend the initial part of the day watching TV or generally idling about. Come evening, he would step out all energized and rejuvenated to hit one or the other among his favoured bars. If he didn't already have a pretty woman for company, he would be on a constant lookout for someone he could engage and bring back with him.

But today wasn't going to be just another Sunday. Last evening itself he had instructed members of his support staff – the security guard, the nurse and the cleaning lady – to reach the clinic at their usual time. He wasn't expecting any patients, but there was a crucial surgery he had to carry out the next day, for which he needed to make necessary preparations. Abhigyan had hoped to wrap up his work by the afternoon so that he could still have the evening to himself. But he was already ruing his decision now. At this point, a few additional hours of sleep seemed far more lucrative than an evening of revelry in the company of women and wine. Members of his staff would already be reaching the clinic, he knew, and he needed to join them sooner or later.

Taking one last swig from the cup, he lifted his heavy eyelids to look at the meticulously ticking wall clock – quarter to ten. Fifteen minutes to change and drive down to his clinic, there was no way he was going to make it in time. His employees would wait, they were ordained to, but he needed to get on with it nonetheless. With some effort, he propped himself on his reluctant feet and made for the shower. Negotiating the mixer to a preferred temperature range, with a measured step he surrendered himself to the deluge of steaming droplets. The warm gush felt invigorating.

In some time he emerged, rubbing his hair vigorously with the towel in his hand, looking restored and ready. He had only reached out for the first piece of clothing, one that would absolve him of his state of utter nakedness, when his mobile decided to come alive. 'Must be the clinic,' he thought, sparing a look of annoyance for the incessantly buzzing handset. He had no intentions of taking the call. Not until his mind deciphered the digital alphabets making up the name of the caller at least.

The name made him leap. Well, almost. And in no time he was clutching the phone to make sure that his eyes had not deceived him. It wasn't usual for her to call. In fact, she had hardly ever called him. It was always him calling her, thinking of her, trying to meet her. 'She is probably returning my call, at her father's behest of course,' the saner part of him argued even as he slid his finger on the screen and lifted the phone to his ears.

'Hi, how are you?' her voice hit him like a lyrical chime.

'Hey, now that's what I call a pleasant surprise! I have been fine…,' he began, trying desperately to contain his excitement. Over the next few sentences it became evident that she wasn't merely returning his call. In fact, she had called to confide in him, to seek his help – like a confidante, a friend. Abhigyan was euphoric. The clinic, his waiting staffers, they were all suddenly an obscure abstraction. The only reality that remained was that she had called to seek his help. She needed him, and that to him was the beginning of the answer to his prayers.

'Of course you can have the money… Whatever belongs to me is yours too, and you can choose to use it as you please,' he heard himself saying. His surge of emotions was getting the better of him and he had to check himself before he scared her away. He needed to deftly steer the conversation in the direction he wanted, and that he managed with effortless ease. Before the line was disconnected, he had arranged to meet Sargam at his clinic that very afternoon. 'From there we will head someplace quiet for a peaceful drink,' he had added for good measure, and the suggestion had gone down without an objection. Today was the day perhaps, the day he had been waiting so desperately for.

The need to get to his clinic had become even more urgent now. He had to complete his work and be ready for her when she arrived. The eagerness was palpable, adding a spring to his steps and a sense of urgency to his actions. As he stood in front of the wardrobe-mirror, dressing up, he realized that the conversation with Sargam and the expectations it had fuelled had had the most visible impact on a certain part of his anatomy which he was now attempting to cover. A crooked smile involuntarily escaped his lips.

In half the usual time, Dr. Abhigyan Kukreti found himself in his car, racing through the light Sunday traffic towards his clinic. There was but one person on his mind – Sargam. Like a seasoned filmmaker he was scripting the scene of their rendezvous within his head, using his imagination to populate the frames to the minutest of details, and returning to the drawing board as soon as he spotted an opportunity to better himself. He was hardly thinking about the surgery he was to perform the next day, the ailing patient whose life lay in his hands, or her devout and loving son Junaid, who had left no stone unturned to see his mother back on her feet again.

Junaid Akhtar

The Santro car, like an inconsequential speck in the Monday evening deluge of vehicles, was slowly but surely carving its way towards its destination. At the wheel was Sanjay, a buoyant young man in his late twenties. Sitting alongside was a girl, roughly the same age as him, clad in an elegant Lucknowi suit, toying laboriously with one corner of her dupatta. Sanjay stole a quick glance at her and smiled to himself over her preoccupation of the past several minutes. She was visibly nervous – a good sign as far as he was concerned.

It wasn't just her, the air within the rolled-up windows of the car was tense too. So much so that both the occupants had hardly noticed when the radio, from doling out romantic melodies had moved on to reviewing the last set of Bollywood presentations to have hit the theatres. The radio had clearly failed to draw them from their thoughts, and that wasn't surprising.

The two had come in contact about four months ago through a matrimonial website. They hadn't exactly hit it off like a house on fire, but for some inexplicable reason they had opted to remain in touch. Perhaps it was the unspoken mutual acceptance that their union was not to be, but soon the veil of formalities and expectations had weathered and their relationship had adorned the garb of friendship. It was this firm and guileless bond to have unwittingly developed between them that had forced Sanjay to re-evaluate Jharna against the original motive that had brought them together. She came out with flying colours. And today, following his invite, Jharna had agreed to meet him over a cup of coffee – their first ever tete-a-tete.

Sanjay had received her at the pre-designated bus stand in Uttam Nagar and they were now heading towards a shopping mall in Rajouri Garden for the cups of promised coffee. Jharna, Sanjay noticed, was far more attractive than her photographs made her out to be, and she was barely half as forthcoming in person as she had been in the digital space – both observations only reinforcing the correctness of his decision to ask her out. He was gloating in anxious anticipation and clearly Jharna was nervous too.

'What the…,' he nearly screamed, as a motorbike overtook his car from the left and, cutting across the lane in dangerous proximity of his front bumper, squeezed ahead in the narrow space between the divider on the extreme right and the crawling vehicles adjacent to it. The rider had appeared to be gesticulating towards the Santro's bonnet, but he had crossed past in such jiffy that Sanjay was unsure if he had been trying to draw his attention towards something or was simply asking to be allowed through. As he let out a gasp and looked at Jharna, he found her staring right back at him. Thankfully he had managed to truncate his verbal riposte to the motorcyclist's act, for the word ready to drop from his lips would certainly have diluted his candidature in Jharna's eyes. Cussing other motorists, no matter how justified the reason, wasn't the best tactic to impress a pretty girl after all.

Barely a few minutes later the car was once again rendered motionless by one of the many traffic signals peppering their path. Impervious to Sanjay's mounting impatience, the signal took its time in changing shades. And just as it turned green, allowing him to set the vehicle in motion, he was forced to press hard on the brakes again. A man, hitherto twiddling with his mobile phone on the pavement had suddenly decided to cross the road. Sanjay once again found several expletives racing through his vocal cords, but somehow managed to keep them from spilling, opting instead to express his displeasure by resting his palm on the car horn. The man, as he crossed the Santro, looked at the car's bonnet and then at Sanjay, his forehead creasing in a concerned frown. Catching Sanjay's eye he said something, pointing towards the car's engine, but his words failed to rise above the din of traffic and the blaring horn to seep within the closed confines of the car.

In the little time it took Sanjay to let go of his immediate frustrations and realize that the man had been trying to tell him something, he had already crossed the road and was briskly striding away from him. The stranger had soon gone out of sight, but Sanjay was curiously concerned now. Once could have been a mistake, but not twice. There surely was something unusual on the car that was visible to passersby but not him. Alarmed, he began negotiating the vehicle leftwards and after about fifty yards, was able to bring the car to a complete halt. Instructing Jharna to remain seated, he got down to inspect the vehicle.

'What happened, why is the engine sparking?' a bystander enquired, stepping towards Sanjay.

'Sparks? Were there sparks emanating from the engine? I didn't see them,' Sanjay shot back, more out of fear than anything else. He had read several news reports about vehicles catching fire and claiming the lives of their occupants lately, and the last thing he wanted was to be found charred alongside the girl he was hoping to settle down with.

'Strange! The vehicle nearly left a trail of sparks behind and you didn't even notice! Why don't you open the bonnet and see what's wrong?'

Dumbfounded, Sanjay found merit in the man's suggestion and returning to the driving side of the vehicle, pulled the lever meant to open the bonnet. By the time he stepped out, the man – a Good Samaritan – was already holding the car's hood over his head and peering into the engine. Sanjay joined him. He didn't rate his own understanding of vehicular engineering very highly and in little time it was obvious that the helpful stranger was no proficient mechanic either. Between them they had failed to spot anything out of place to which they could attribute the sparking.

'Why don't you start the engine once… Let's see if it is still sparking,' the man suggested once again, and Sanjay complied. But within seconds of turning the ignition on, he was forced to shut it back again. He could see the sparks now – angry and threatening – emerging from somewhere within the engine. The petrol tank was not too far from the flying sparks.

'This needs a mechanic,' the man muttered. 'There is a small shop nearby that I know of; I will be passing it on my way from here. If you want I can show you to it,' he further offered. Sanjay, still emerging from the motions of thanking his stars for saving him from a certain and grotesque end, was glad to latch on to the offer. Instructing Jharna to remain seated, he started following the helpful stranger. They were heading towards the mouth of a narrow by lane just across the road.

'Oh, the shop seems to be shut today,' the man apologetically remarked, as they reached a nondescript small shanty with its shutters pulled down. There were no boards, no signages, only a few discarded vehicles parked in the small patch of barren land adjacent to it.

'What do you want?' as though sensing their discomfort, another man emerged from behind one of the parked vehicles to address them. He was holding a spanner in his hand and the grease stains on his clothes came as a welcome sight for Sanjay.

'We were looking for a car mechanic,' the stranger guiding Sanjay was the first to speak.

'Come back tomorrow, the shop is closed today… I had just come to finish some pending work, none of my boys are in today,' he replied dismissively. To Sanjay, this man was a knight in shining armour. He couldn't let go of him. And so, he began pleading for him to spare a few minutes and look at his car. 'It is not too far, just outside this lane on the main road,' he said.

While the mechanic pondered over the situation, the stranger who had led Sanjay to the shop gave him a slight tap on the shoulder. 'I must get going,' he said, and without giving Sanjay a chance to express his gratitude, was on his way.

The mechanic, after displaying a certain degree of reluctance, accompanied Sanjay back to the car. A brief inspection of the engine and turning the ignition key on and off a couple of times was all it took for him to diagnose the problem. 'It is the Alternator. It will need to be replaced,' he declared.

'How long will it take? And how much will it cost?' Sanjay shot back.

'It costs near about six thousand rupees. If you want it replaced, I could call a nearby automobile spare parts store and have them deliver it right here. Fifteen to twenty minutes at most…'

He didn't have many options left. The unexpected breakdown had already eaten into most of his time with Jharna, and if the meeting was still to be salvaged, he needed to get moving at the earliest. However, he couldn't just take the mechanic's words on face value. Although Sanjay himself didn't understand the components of a car engine, alternators and the likes included, the price the mechanic had quoted was not meagre by any standards. So, he stepped to the side and dialled his regular mechanic's number before coming up with a definitive answer.

'Raju, Sanjay here… The Santro, yes…Tell me, what will be the approximate price of a new alternator?'

'You are getting it changed or what?' the mechanic, sensing a loss of business, shot back.

'No, no, one of my friends has had a breakdown. He was checking with me, so I thought I will ask you.'

'Oh ok… Ask him to come to my shop and give your reference then, I will get it done for the lowest price possible. In the market it will cost him anywhere between seven to eight thousand rupees, but since he is your friend, I will do it for six-and-a-half,' he replied. Sanjay had got the information he needed, and so, assuring Raju that he would certainly share his shop's address with this imaginary friend, he disconnected the call. The confirmation that an alternator did indeed cost in the vicinity of the price that had been quoted to him did not dissuade Sanjay from engaging in a further bit of haggling, and much to his delight, he managed to secure the deal for five thousand and eight hundred rupees, inclusive of the mechanic's fees.

The mechanic proved true to his word and minutes after Sanjay had returned from a nearby ATM machine after withdrawing the required amount of cash, a boy showed up with a replacement for the faulty part. Once the part was replaced, the vehicle came to life with just a slight twist of the ignition key. The threatening sparks had now disappeared. Sanjay and Jharna were soon on their way, expressing their shared gratitude to the bunch of strangers who had saved them from the jaws of death by averting the mishap they were to be at the epicentre of. The flow of romance within their hearts, which had been interrupted, was once again surging to take control of their senses.

It would be a few days later, when Sanjay, compelled by another breakdown to visit his regular mechanic, would learn that the supposedly faulty part to have been replaced that day was not the alternator but a mere eight hundred rupees worth ignition coil. He had been conned and the perpetrators had not only made off with his money, but also replaced his original ignition coil with a cheap replica that was designed to last no more than a couple of days.

'What about the sparks then? I had seen them with my own eyes,' a distraught Sanjay had further quizzed Raju, the mechanic.

'Oh, that's simple. He must have pulled this wire here and loosened this knob… like this… when you went back to the driving seat to turn on the ignition,' the mechanic had replied, moving on to demonstrate the mechanics behind the cleverly crafted con. 'It has become a common fraud these days and I am getting 2-3 customers every week who have been cheated in similar fashion. Had you told me the details when you spoke to me that day, I would have warned you.'

◆

'Here,' he said, handing over two crisp five-hundred rupee notes to the young boy who had promptly arrived with the replacement part for Sanjay's car. 'Don't blow it all on Hashish, save some for a bad day,' he added for good measure.

They were five in all – the motorcyclist, the pedestrian, the samaritan, the mechanic and the boy. Their leader, the samaritan, was doling out their shares of the spoils to them at a roadside tea-stall, not far from the crime scene. There was no imminent danger in sticking close to the crime scene, they knew, for it wouldn't be before a couple of days that the victim would even realize that he had been duped. This was how it played out, each time, without fail.

'What are you saying Junaid bhai? I don't smoke anymore,' the boy replied with a sheepish grin. The denial was feeble, and it warranted no more than a stare from Junaid.

Sanjay, had he witnessed the Junaid of now – an antithesis to the eager and helpful citizen he had been a short while back – would have found it hard to believe his eyes. Junaid, in his speech, actions and disposition was now a shrewd and sly man of the world, the undisputed leader of the bunch of thugs. 'Tomorrow morning, same place then,' he directed, surrendering his own share of the booty – two thousand rupees – to his thoroughly worn-out denims.

He had opened his mouth to add something when his mobile phone buzzed to life. 'Hello,' he received the call, a frown emerging on his forehead at the sight of the number flashing on the screen. 'Oh… okay… yes… I am coming right away, you stay there please,' he said, the frown giving way to a look of grave concern. 'I need to rush home. Ammi has had another one of her acute attacks of abdominal pain,' he said to no one in particular before making for the nearby bus stop in brisk strides.

Junaid had been born and brought up in the cluster of slums adjoining the Okhla Industrial Estate. The cluster – if ever a ranking of such nefarious and gloomy dwelling constellations across the city were to be undertaken on counts of poverty and impoverishment – would have emerged a strong contender for the top slot. The nearby Industrial Estate and the Fruit Market offered employment to some of its dwellers in the form of daily-wage labourers, cart pullers and other such, but that was merely a drop in the ocean. Majority of households from the cluster, including Junaid's, had no dependable source of income and subsisted in extremely pitiable and pathetic conditions.

Junaid had never seen his father. As a child he had been told that the man had gone to Gujarat in search of better employment opportunities. He had believed this argument, but only until his mind had honed itself sufficiently to understand the ways of the world. His father, wherever he was, had not come back till then and was never going to come back either. In fact, he wasn't even sure if there was any one man who could be attributed the blame of having sired him. Life in the slums wasn't easy and he had grown up watching morality and values being mercilessly trampled under the weight of an empty stomach. Hunger, he had learnt, was the closest aide of the Devil, if not the Devil himself. He had seen people do strange, unimaginable things under its influence, and his Ammi was in no way insulated from it.

The one person who, since his earliest recollections, had remained unwaveringly by his side had been his Ammi. He had seen her borrowing chapatis from neighbours to ensure that he didn't have to sleep empty stomach; he had seen her spend nights after night sitting upright with his head in her lap when he had been unwell; and when the other children were busy playing in the mucky streets, he had seen her strive to send him to the nearby municipal school. 'You will become a big man one day and rescue us both from this hell,' she would often say to him.

It was her tenacity that made him persist with the school till the fifth standard – just about all he could endure of the country's formal education system. There were two immediate reasons for his dropping out of school. First, he had failed his fifth standard examinations and would have had to repeat the year – a humiliation he was not prepared to endure. And second, the realization that his mother's meagre income from washing utensils in a few nearby homes could either support their stomach or his education, not both.

However, he didn't immediately have the nerve to confide in his Ammi about his dropping out of school. He was scared of her possible reactions to the news. So, he started stepping out of the house every morning like he always did, giving her the impression that his routine remained uncompromised, and whiling away time on the bustling Delhi roads. This went on for nearly six months. Thereafter, when his Ammi did come to know of the deliberate abandoning of his educational pursuits, her reaction was as volatile as Junaid had expected. She stewed, she cursed, she cried, but she could no longer correct the damage that had been done.

The strain in their relationship lingered for weeks, and Junaid, overcome by guilt, kept looking for odd jobs that would give him enough cash to bring home a small present or two. A new sari, slippers – a replacement for her shabby and badly tattered ones, or even a spicy samosa that he was able to bring back for her, satisfied him like no other thing could. This was about the time that Junaid found his purpose in life: to make loads of money, no matter what the means.

His brush with the proscribed began when he realized the value of metallic vehicle logos in the black market. A small metal strip was all he needed, and by simply hovering around unmanned car parks he was able to extract 4 to 5 logos within a working hour – a booty worth anywhere between five hundred to a thousand rupees depending upon the model and make of the cars. He got caught in the act a few times too, but his age kept him from getting into serious trouble each time. A reprimand and sometimes a few lofty blows, depending on the evidence in his possession and the circumstances under which he had been apprehended, these were hardly punitive enough to make him mend his ways.

With time his brashness only increased and soon he found himself at the helm of a gang of delinquents, much like his own self. Junaid, with his sharp mind and clever ideas kept coming up with schemes and plots to help them make money, and the others were only glad to follow his lead. He would come up with ideas that posed little risk and were easily implementable and replicable. As soon as their modus operandi became common knowledge or the authorities woke up to their existence, they would lie low for some time and resurface with an entirely novel scheme.

While Junaid remained surrounded by his gang of wrongdoers most of the time, the only constructive influence in his life other than his Ammi was Ajay, a childhood friend who lived three houses from his own in the same slum cluster. Ajay and Junaid had started attending school around the same time, and while Junaid had taken the easier way out, Ajay had braved all odds to earn a graduation degree for himself. He was now employed as a peon with a private firm in Okhla, a highly revered engagement by the prevailing standards of the neighbourhood.

Whenever Junaid could, he would seek Ajay's company and chat with him for hours over mundane matters. Initially Ajay had tried counselling him into mending his ways, but to no avail. He had given up eventually, accepting their relationship for what it was – friendship between two individuals, dissimilar in their thought and outlook. To Junaid, Ajay was his window to the world. Simply listening to him talk, hearing his views on matters larger than his own shallow existence – the prevailing political tidings for instance – was a much treasured source of intellectual workout for him. It wouldn't be wrong to say that in a lot of ways Junaid looked up to Ajay, but at the same time had stubbornly shut himself to following in his footsteps.

All appeared to be going well for Junaid, at least by the measure of his own script for life, till his Ammi suffered her first bout of abdominal pain. It was a tearing, intense pain that lasted for about ten excruciating minutes, making the old lady wince and scream in agony. Junaid had been at home then and he, like his mother, had hoped that it was a one-off display of abdominal resistance to a disagreeable ingestion of some sort. Their hopes were however quelled over the next few days. The pain persisted, returning in frequent bouts, more fervent and lengthier than the preceding ones. Even the pungent smelling, brown paste the Hakim had prescribed for application on the abdomen thrice a day seemed utterly incapable of assuaging her agony.

On Ajay's insistence and against his Ammi's vehement disapproval, Junaid eventually managed to coax her into visiting a nearby dispensary to see a doctor. The doctor prescribed his own set of medicines which proved just as ineffective as the Hakim's herbal paste in containing the ailment. After changing the medication twice, he too was forced to concede and referred her case to the government hospital. Junaid's life, from its erstwhile placidity had suddenly turned tense and turbulent. It was the doctor at the hospital, who, after several diagnostic tests surmised that the patient needed to undergo an operation to remove her gallbladder.

The operation not being of urgent nature, Junaid was forced to register his Ammi in the unusually long waiting-list of patients in need of surgical interventions, and await his turn. The resources at the disposal of the hospital were expectedly scarce and it was only after an agonizing wait of over three months that his turn finally came. Those were anxious days for Junaid. His mother meant the world to him, and the very image of her lying on a surgical table, being sliced open by a bunch of masked strangers was unnerving to say the least. But Junaid braced himself and went ahead, drawing strength from the thought that it was all for his Ammi's well-being. He waited in the crammed waiting area of the hospital, unmindful of the stench surrounding him – of the government-supplied, crude disinfectant mingled with the more human odors of perspiration, pain and panic – till he saw his mother being wheeled out of the Operation Theatre towards the General Ward. The operation, the Doctor conveyed, had been successful and he could hope to return home with his Ammi within a couple of days.

'I am feeling much better now... lighter and untroubled,' she had said to Junaid on regaining consciousness, words that justified all his endurances of the past months. On the third day she was discharged from the hospital and Junaid brought her back home, hopeful that her nemesis had been put to rest for good. The reprieve persisted too, for a fortnight nearly, before the pain resurfaced in a nastier, harsher avatar. And once it had returned, it kept coming back, in intense, stinging bouts, making his ailing mother wither and wince in agony. It seemed as if her innards had decided to avenge the intrusion she had subjected them to. Sometimes she would scream too, the gut-wrenching wail known to stretch the frontiers of human tolerance, and Junaid would feel something sharp slithering through his own helpless being as well.

Only the previous day he had committed the last of his savings to his Ammi's ailment, taking her to a renowned private hospital for a check-up. The orderly and hygienic surroundings and even the staff's deportment was a sharp contrast to the hospitals he had hitherto known, and this had inspired a sense of confidence in him. The confidence was only bolstered when he met the doctor, an amiable man whose concern for his mother's health appeared genuine. Tests were done, reports prepared, and the pronouncement was finally made – those morons at the government hospital had goofed up her earlier surgery and caused some sort of an internal injury to his Ammi. The injury, Jamal gathered, was serious and it warranted an immediate corrective surgery.

It was only when he figured the cost of such a surgery that his optimism began to wane. He begged and pleaded with the doctor, and though he succeeded in convincing the kind man to carry out the surgery at his own clinic for a significantly lower sum, the amount still remained beyond Junaid's limited means.

As he left the hospital premises, Junaid was struggling with a barrage of diverse emotions. He felt a strong urge to confront the man whose ineptitude had led to his Ammi's present condition and strangulate him with his bare hands. He felt like hiding himself somewhere and crying over his helplessness. He saw flashy cars and well-dressed men on the streets and felt a sudden pang of hatred towards them – would they ever know what it was like to not be able to afford the treatment cost for a dear one? His thoughts had continued to haunt him through the night, and come morning he had set out to do the one thing he could – make money.

The racket his gang was engaged in these days was an improvisation of an idea that Junaid had read somewhere. The trick was novel, and given the sea of vehicles plying on Delhi roads each day, they could very nearly pick their targets at will. And if each of them stuck to their assigned roles, there was hardly a chance that their prey would suspect anything untoward until much after the con had been staged. In fact most of their victims showered them with gratitude for having saved their lives before they happily left. It was a perfect scheme for his lot, and it would have been for him too if it weren't for his mother's illness. The money was just not enough to meet his immediate needs, and this was the thought racing through his mind as he pocketed his share of two thousand rupees when the call informing him of his mother having suffered yet another attack came through.

Junaid rushed home, apprehensive and scared, to be by his Ammi's side in her moment of agony. But the moment had long gone by the time the city's public transport network could successfully deliver him to his destination. His Ammi had taken her pills and was sound asleep when Junaid stepped inside the shanty. Jaya Chachi, Ajay's mother, was at her bedside, nearly asleep herself.

'It was pretty bad… I was washing utensils when I heard her screams. I rushed here immediately and called you… It lasted for about ten minutes before subsiding on its own… She took her medicines and slept off about half an hour back,' Chachi, on spotting Junaid, gave him a quick recount of all that he had missed before making for the door. 'In case you are hungry, I have made some chawal-dal,' she added as an afterthought – an invite that Junaid politely turned down. Food was the last thing on his mind right then. The peace of sleep wasn't enough to mask the sufferings of his Ammi and Junaid could already feel something turn within his stomach at the sight.

He remained seated at her bedside for a while, lovingly stroking her hair and massaging her forehead, before abruptly getting up and heading towards the part of the room where the soot-blackened stove stood. It was nearly dinner time and although he didn't feel the need for food, he had to prepare something lest Ammi were to get up feeling hungry.

The khichadi was nearly done when Ajay stepped in, calling aloud his name just as he always did – more an announcement of his own arrival than an enquiry of Junaid's whereabouts. 'Ma told me about Chachi. How is she feeling now?' he inquired, eyeing the scrawny figure sprawled on the metal cot. Junaid did not answer; he only shrugged his shoulders helplessly.

'Come, let's walk to Roshan's and grab a cup of tea. The outside air should do you some good,' Ajay offered, presumably due to the misery and despair he saw writ large on his friend's face. Junaid refused initially, unsure whether he should step out before his Ammi was awake, but Ajay would have none of it. In a few minutes they were occupying two rickety stools at the neighbourhood roadside tea-stall, holding cups of the steaming brew.

'For how long can this go on… how long can I continue eking out a meagre living this way? Something needs to be done… and soon.' It was Junaid who punctured their private silence. And once the ampoule containing his emotions had been breached, they came tumbling out unrestrained. Ajay listened wordlessly as Junaid poured his heart out to him, painting a picture of melancholic gloom with his words.

'I know I have been less than an ideal son, but why should my Ammi be the one to pay for my sins? She has never wronged anyone in her entire life… I won't let her die such a painful death, no matter what it takes.' Junaid went on and on as Ajay listened in rapt attention. He knew that the one thing his friend needed most was a willing ear, and he was glad to be able to offer his.

'I have some money in the bank, fifteen thousand rupees or so. You can have that if it helps…,' he managed to interrupt the monologue to slip in his two bits at one point, nearly bringing Junaid to tears.

'Thanks Ajay,' Junaid replied, reaching out to briefly hold Ajay's hand in a gesture that conveyed more than what a full-blown embrace ever could. 'The one person I know I can always count on is you, but fifteen thousand is not going to be enough. I need a much larger sum, nearly a lakh rupees…'

After a brief pause to allow the enormity of his need to sink in, he resumed, 'But don't worry! I am going to get the money somehow. Anyhow. I don't have a plan as yet, but there will soon be one. And even if it turns out to be the last heist I ever pull off, I am going to get the money. I owe this to Ammi.'

Ajay had almost opened his mouth to let Junaid know his views on the means he was contemplating for raising the money, but he checked himself at the last minute. This was neither the time nor the occasion to deliver a sermon on righteousness and honesty. If ever he were to be in Junaid's place, there was little doubt that he too would choose his mother's wellbeing over morality and principles.

They remained chatting for over an hour. Ajay was hungry, but the hunger was more bearable than the thought of asking Junaid to stop. It was only after he had said all that he had to, repeating some of the things many times over, that he realized the need to get back home to his Ammi. The two friends walked back in complete silence, Ajay choosing to walk Junaid to his shanty first. The old lady was asleep, just as they had left her, and Ajay quietly slipped out, leaving Junaid to deal with his demons. In less than twelve hours Junaid would realize the significance of this seemingly futile chat he had engaged in with his friend.

◆

'Yes, it's me. I have some information for you, but I will share it only on one condition...'

'What?'

Junaid was perplexed. It wasn't usual for Ajay to call him at such an early hour, a time when he was presumably at work. Moreover, the information...the condition...he was alluding to, didn't make any sense to him. He glanced at the watch strapped to his wrist – 10:50 a.m.

'The condition is that this will be the last heist you ever pull off, just as you had said yesterday... Once Chachi's operation is taken care of, you will look for a job and earn an honest living. Are you up for it?'

The suspense as well as Junaid's confusion was mounting. 'What are you referring to? Which heist and what job? I am not getting you,' he said.

'I have some information that can help you get the money you need for Chachi's operation. In return I need you to promise me that you will mend your ways and give up this life of a petty crook. You think you can do that?'

Suddenly Ajay had all of Junaid's attention. He got up and stepped away from the rest of his group. The gang of five was seated at their usual meeting point – a nondescript dhaba in Munirka village – running through the shortlist of locations to identify the one where they would stage their well-rehearsed act today.

'What kind of information?' he hissed, checking his volume. The dialogue had suddenly acquired enough importance to be accorded a veil of privacy.

'The promise first!'

'Fine, if indeed the information you possess helps me get the money I need, I promise, I will give up all my nefarious engagements once and for all. Now tell me...'

For the next few minutes Junaid kept listening to what Ajay had to say. 'I think it's workable,' he eventually said, excitement discernible in his voice. 'We will be ready to greet him. You just keep an eye on him and let me know whenever he leaves... and thank you for this. It means a lot!'

It took little time for Junaid to dismiss the gang, all but Sunil, his most trusted lieutenant and the only member of the group who owned a motorbike.

Ajay had told Junaid that his employer had withdrawn one lakh rupees from the bank that morning and that he intended to deliver it to a customer sometime during the day. Ajay didn't know the whereabouts or the time of the intended meeting, but was confident that he would be able to keep a watch on his boss and inform Junaid whenever he left the office. All Junaid needed to do was follow and apprehend him at the opportune time and the money could be his for the taking.

The plot had certain inherent risks too: What if the venue of the meeting was someplace close to the office or in a location which wouldn't require him to cross any desolate stretches? What if the man refused to hand over the money and decided to put up a fight? But his need far outweighed the concerns, and Sunil in tow, Junaid was soon stationed at a spot across the road from Ajay's office. All he needed to do now was wait and hope that Ajay was able to acquire all the information that Junaid required to stake his claim on the money.

The wait proved longer than he had anticipated and it was only towards the evening that he once again heard from Ajay. Ajay's call was brief, but with each word he spoke, the smile on Junaid's face only widened. Not only had he managed to find out the name of the hotel where the meeting was to take place and the precise description of the packet that contained the money, but he also informed Junaid that the boss, instead of going to meet the client himself, had relegated the task to a female employee of his. Ajay had been around when the girl had been summoned by the boss, and stationing himself near the file-cabinet adjacent to his cabin, he had been able to acquire all the details that he had shared with Junaid.

The hotel where the girl was to deliver the money wasn't too far from the office, but there was an arterial road leading to the hotel entrance that was just right for executing their plan without the risk of drawing much unwanted attention. The girl was likely to be travelling in an auto rickshaw, an easier vehicle to forcibly stop than a car, and being an employee herself, not the owner of the packet in her possession, she wasn't expected to put up much of a fight either. It was all shaping up even better than what Junaid had been hoping for.

If Junaid had thought that he had exhausted his quota of good fortune for the day, he was in for another pleasant surprise. He didn't even have to risk a confrontation for claiming the packet that contained the solution to his immediate problem. The girl, in all her naivety, had stopped the rickshaw mid-way and got down to buy a bouquet, leaving her purse unattended. This was as good an opportunity as any and both Junaid and Sunil were practiced enough to not let it pass. While Sunil engaged the driver in a conversation, Junaid was dexterously able to extract the packet from her purse. They had once again managed a clean take without as much as alarming their victim.

That very evening Junaid made a quick trip to the doctor's clinic and deposited the advance for his Ammi's operation. Only a day stood between his mother and the cure to her sufferings now. And of course destiny!

29th December

Sargam was in her room, pulling out dresses from her wardrobe, scrutinizing them and lackadaisically returning them to where they had been pulled out from. It wasn't the yearning to look her best, but her disinclination towards the meeting she had herself scheduled which was responsible for the unusually long time she was taking to settle on a dress to wear. After lunch she had whiled away some time watching TV and only when she could delay no more did she drag herself to her room.

She was holding up a peach-coloured Chikan salwar-suit when her phone screamed for attention. Excavating it from beneath a heap of garments piled up on the bed, she looked at its flashing screen. It was an unknown landline number. Reluctantly she received the call, nearly certain that it was some target-driven enthusiast trying to sell her a vacation package or a credit card.

'Madam Joshi?' a gruff and business-like voice enquired instead.

'Yes, that's me,' she muttered.

'I am calling from the Srinivaspuri Police Station. You had come here a few hours back to lodge a complaint?'

'Yes'

'Can you come down to the Police Station right away?' The man was struggling to make his words sound like a request rather than an order. He wasn't perhaps accustomed to holding conversations with many people on the right side of the law, let alone a suave and soft-spoken girl.

'What's the matter? Why do I need to come to the Police Station?' Sargam retorted, somewhat alarmed.

'We have the fellow who stole your money here, and we need you to identify him.' The words fell into her ears like droplets of warm mustard oil, soothing and revitalizing.

'I will be right there,' was all she could mutter.

'Ask for PSI Sangram Singh once you reach,' he replied, abruptly disconnecting the call thereafter.

In about twenty minutes of the call, Sargam was stepping inside the Srinivaspuri Police Station for a second time within a space of few hours. She asked for the PSI and was summarily directed towards a corridor with three open doors on one side and a series of wooden benches lining the opposing wall. The benches were all occupied and Sargam had to settle for standing against the wall between two doors, one among them bearing the name of PSI Sangram Singh.

She was curious and excited. There was a ray of hope that her ordeal might be on its last leg and she wanted to breeze past this final hurdle towards inner peace and quietude. But her hopes and wishes had little bearing on the pace at which matters were being dealt with at the police station. She kept leaning against the wall and awaiting her turn till her legs began to ache. Thankfully, that was around when two men from the bench facing her were summoned inside one of the rooms. Sargam darted to replace one of them, and her wait resumed, only in a somewhat more comfortable state.

'Joshi,' she heard someone call out from within one of the rooms. At first the name failed to register. She had been addressed by several variations of her name in the past, but this was a first. It was when no one else responded to the call that the realization dawned. It was she who was being summoned. She gathered herself hastily and made for the door.

The room wasn't anything like the personal cabins she was accustomed to seeing in the corporate world. There were three wooden tables placed in L-shape to make full use of the available space. Each had bundles of ancient-looking files and papers placed atop, and three men, two of them in uniform, occupied the chairs behind them. It was difficult to tell who among them was the man she sought. There were also several others who were freely moving about the room, chit-chatting and cracking jokes, lending the room an air of a community hall rather than a place of serious business. Nervously she approached the first table and announced herself. The man looked up from the sheet he had been furiously scribbling on, eyed her momentarily and wordlessly gestured towards the last table, the biggest among the three.

'Come, come... So you are the one whose money was stolen,' PSI Sangram Singh greeted her as she approached his table. The voice was unmistakable. This was the man who had called her earlier. As she nodded in acknowledgement, her phone once again began to buzz. She hurriedly disconnected the call without bothering to look at the screen to ascertain the caller's identity.

'Sit, sit,' the elderly petite man, a sharp contrast to the image Sargam's mind had constructed of him, said. She gladly parked herself on one of the two wooden chairs facing him. 'Get the guy,' he instructed no one in particular, and Sargam noticed one of the meandering men quietly exit the room.

'So, the money was stolen last evening?' the man said, pulling out a sheet of paper which Sargam identified as the one where her complaint had been recorded that morning. The question was a mere rhetoric; the man probably wanted her to repeat the entire sequence of events to him. Just as she was starting to speak, her phone went off again. Annoyed with the distraction, she disconnected the call and switched off the instrument for good measure. She then went on to narrate the entire episode from the time she had left office to the discovery that the packet was missing from her purse. PSI Singh listened attentively without a single interjection.

'What denomination were the notes?' he asked after a punctuating silence.

'The notes...I didn't see them. I never opened the packet... But if you want I can check with my employer. He was the one to have handed over the packet to me,' she clarified.

'No, I don't think that will be necessary,' he said, shifting his eyes towards the door mid-sentence. Sargam followed his gaze, and what she saw made her heart skip a beat.

A policeman had just entered the room, his hands locked with that of another man who was trailing right behind. It was the sight of this other man that had made Sargam gasp. His dishevelled hair was muddy and there were fresh scars all across his face and body. One of his eyes was swollen and a purplish tinge was gathering around it. His clothes were ragged and only two of his shirt buttons remained to preserve his modesty. A whitish, dried trail connected the edge of his lips to his chin – vomit or saliva perhaps that the man had failed to wipe in time. What perturbed Sargam the most was that the man looked vaguely familiar. He looked quite like

Sharib, the man who had been ferrying her to office and back till just the previous evening.

'Here, this is what we found on him,' the policeman escorting the man said, dropping something on the table with a thud. Sargam's eyes automatically darted towards the source of the sound and she saw a bundle of thousand rupee notes sitting between PSI Sangram Singh and her.

'Is he the man who stole your money?' PSI Singh asked her. Sargam wasn't able to voice a response instantaneously; it was all happening too fast for her comprehension. Perhaps gauging her situation, the PSI added, 'We picked him from his residence around the afternoon today. He had ninety-five thousand rupees in his possession, the rest he might have spent last evening itself. He hasn't confessed to the crime yet – they never do – but that is purely a matter of time. A few days of police hospitality and he will be singing like a koyal.'

If anything, the PSI's words did well to quash any traces of pity that had begun to emerge within her at the sight of the pulped man. Instead, her own misery, her anguish of the past 24 hours came rushing back like a torrential downpour, filling the crevices of her mind with violent rage and loathing. She turned to look at Sharib who stood still like a lifeless mannequin. This was the man who had betrayed her, pushed her to a point where she had very nearly been compelled to compromise her values and ethics. He deserved anything but mercy. For a splitting instance her gaze caught his stony eyes, but she was quick to disengage it.

'Yes, that's him,' she said emphatically.

Sharib didn't utter a word. He kept looking at her dumbfounded, as a sheep might do at the sight of the same man who has painstakingly reared her, polishing his axe. It seemed as if he wanted to say something to her, but no words emerged from his parched lips. And then, the policeman who had escorted him into the room tugged at his arm and took him away. Sargam was in no mood to listen to him either.

'There is some paperwork to be completed before you can claim the money,' PSI Singh said, bringing her back to the present.

After nearly forty minutes, when Sargam emerged from the police station, she had a spring to her strides. In her bag she had ninety thousand rupees – five thousand, out of the recovered amount, she had graciously handed over to PSI Sangram Singh as a token of appreciation for his efforts – and a quick stop at the ATM on the way to work the next morning would allow her to live up to the commitment she had made to Ramamurthy. She might not be heading towards joblessness after all, at least not as yet.

There were several thoughts darting through her jubilant mind, but two individuals perceptibly missing from them were Sharib Sheikh and Dr. Abhigyan Kukreti.

◆

By the time Abhigyan reached his clinic, basic preparations for the surgery had already been made – advantages of having staff members who knew their job well. Not being one to relinquish control, he got down to inspecting every little tool and device himself, not meaning to leave any room for possible errors. It wasn't easy, to get his distracted mind to focus, but when it came to work, Dr. Kukreti was uncompromising.

His support staff did not know, but the doctor was well aware that the surgery he was to perform the next morning was a complicated one. It had become a sort of a professional challenge for him and he couldn't afford to fail. Moreover, his patient and her son had imposed their complete faith in him and it was only fair that he did all he could to put his best foot forward.

Scrutinizing the arrangements didn't take much time and in about twenty minutes he was back on his seat, surveying the case reports. He took his time studying the medical reports, intermittently referring to thick journals and the internet to brush up on aspects of medicine that he thought to be relevant to the case. And once certain that he had done all that he could in terms of prior preparations, he allowed his head to rest on the seat-back and shut his eyes.

The lingering pain in his head was still there, though no longer as excruciating. He carried out a mock run of the next morning's surgery in his mind, just to make sure that he wasn't missing out on anything important, and suddenly his ailing patient's face flashed before him. He pressed some buttons of his mental remote to change the image and in a flash the face changed from an old, ailing one to the young, smiling face of Sargam. 'Cheers,' he heard her say, as she lifted her hand to reveal a champagne flute. A smile inadvertently escaped his lips. Barely a few hours and the image would turn to reality.

'Doctor,' a voice interrupted his reverie. It was his middle-aged Malayali nurse, his assistant since the day he had opened his clinic. Half her head was sticking through the slightly ajar door of his chamber. 'If there isn't anything else to be done, shall I carry on? Peter has invited some friends over for the evening…,' she added.

'Sure Maria, please get going. Just ensure that you are here on time tomorrow.' Not that he had any reasons to cast aspersions on Maria's punctuality, but tomorrow wasn't going to be just another day. Stealing a quick glance at the wall-clock, he added, 'And if Santosh is still around, please do send him in, will you?'

It was already 3:00 and his stomach was grumbling for food. Santosh, the security guard surfaced within moments. Abhigyan pulled out a thousand rupee note from his wallet, and handing it over to him, said, 'Get me a sandwich... and get some lunch for yourself too.'

'Saheb, will we be late? I mean, I had told people at home that I will be back by the afternoon. And the cleaning lady is anyway here...,' Santosh replied grinning sheepishly. It was a Sunday, and although Abhigyan felt somewhat miffed by the lackadaisical approach of his staff, he knew that he couldn't expect much else from them.

'Fine, you can go once you have got the food... get a pack of beers also for me... and get the lady some food too,' he instructed. The beer had been an afterthought. Sargam should have arrived by then, and if she was running late, the beer would do good to keep him company. And in case she happened to turn up anytime soon, he would have something to offer to her – an early start to an evening of promise.

Perhaps driven by the incentive of an early relieving, Santosh returned to the clinic in no time. After handing over the change to Abhigyan, he was relegating the beer cans to the refrigerator when the housekeeping girl came in with his sandwich neatly placed on a plate and a glass of water. Thanking the two, Abhigyan hurriedly grabbed the sandwich. The sight of food already had his stomach screaming and jumping with joy.

Only once he had polished off the sandwich did his thoughts return to Sargam. It was approaching 4:00 and there was still no sign of her. He knew from experience that by calling her – a tacit acceptance of his eagerness to see her – he would only be jeopardizing the plans he had surreptitiously made for the later part of the evening. Women, he knew, craved attention, but only till such time that it was copiously bestowed upon them. Once this craving was satisfied, their interest in its source was very likely to plummet.

But the wait was becoming unbearable with each passing moment. He gave himself 'one beer' – the time he would take to empty one beer can – before he would make the call, and gingerly made for the refrigerator to activate his timer. The optimist in him was hoping that Sargam would materialize before the time ran out, but that was not to be. Junking the empty can in the bin under his table, he reached for his phone and dialled her number. In less than a ring, the phone was summarily disconnected from the other end.

Maybe she's just stepping through the door, he told himself. A few tense moments passed, but he didn't hear the main door open. Another beer, he thought, heading to the refrigerator once again. Ominous thoughts about why Sargam might have disconnected his call began to sprout within his head, but he was quick to quash them. She couldn't cancel the plan. After all she was the one to have called him in the first place. She needed the money, didn't she?

The second beer can was soon brushing shoulders with the first and there was still no news of Sargam. He picked up the phone with trembling hands and dialled her number once again. His heart had already sensed something that his mind was refusing to acknowledge and he could feel a nervous flutter within his belly. It was like watching the horse one has wagered his last penny on, losing its lead in the last strides of the race. He heard half a ring which faded into a long beep. The phone had been disconnected again. This was unacceptable. He was writhing with fury by now. If she was held up with something, the least she could have done was called and informed him. Instinctively, he pressed the redial button on the phone. This time a mechanical voice informed him that the number he was attempting to reach had been switched off.

Exasperated, he stomped his way to the fridge and pulled out a third can. He was no longer thinking straight. The meeting with Sargam had been on his mind ever since he had spoken to her that morning. And in his head he had already painted it as a culmination of his long and patient wait to possess her. She couldn't possibly deprive him of this meeting.

Not left with any alternatives, he dialled her residence number. On the third ring Lalkrishna picked up the phone. Abhigyan was having difficulties talking straight, but he somehow went through the basic courtesies before asking him of Sargam's whereabouts.

'She left home right after lunch, beta. We didn't ask her where she was headed, but she did tell her mother that she will back by the evening. I will ask her to call you once she returns?'

Hadn't he explicitly told her that they would be spending the evening together? How then had she planned to be back home by evening? Unless of course she had no intentions of meeting him right from the time she left her house.

The realization was distressing. He reached out for the beer can, but that was empty too. He made another quick trip to the fridge and beer in hand, slumped down on the chair. He could fret and fume as much as he wanted, but what was the point? He had no control over Sargam or over the situation. He could only pull back to cut his losses now. Perhaps there would be another opportunity, somewhere along the agonizing days of waiting, and he would be able to make all his fantasies count.

For a long time he sat there brooding, arguing with himself and counselling his restless side to treat the situation as only a minor setback. Coming to terms with the situation wasn't easy and even after several jaunts to the refrigerator, the resistance within him wasn't completely quelled.

'Saheb, may I clear the plate,' an unexpected voice interrupted his stream of thoughts. It had come from the housekeeping girl who was standing a step into the chamber, one hand still holding the door ajar behind her.

'Yes, please come in.'

This was the first time he had really set his eyes on the girl. She was in her early twenties and her kohl outlined eyes were big and alive. Her features were sharp, and Abhigyan's practiced eyes could tell that beneath the blue salwar-kameez – her service uniform – was a naturally toned, delightful dusky body.

'What is your name?' he enquired, as she stepped forward allowing the door to shut behind her.

'Saheb, Ameena,' she replied meekly.

'That's an interesting name...And where are you basically from?'

'Azamgarh district.'

'Azamgarh in UP?'

She nodded, reaching out to pick up the empty plate from the table.

'How long have you been in Delhi and where do you stay here?' Abhigyan's charm that had many difficult conquests to its credit was on full display now.

Although alarm bells had begun to sound within her head, Ameena had been taught that when her employer asked her a question, she was meant to answer. So, limiting herself to the minimum number of words she could get away with, she continued replying.

'Oh, that's not long. So, what all have you seen of Delhi? Have you been to India Gate, or the QutabMinar?'

'No saheb, not yet, but I intend to see those places as soon as I am able to take some time off work.'

'Why wait? All you need is someone to show you around. I could do that, you know, show you all the interesting places in the city. There is a restaurant in Old Delhi that serves food prepared by chefs whose forefathers worked the royal kitchens during the Mughal era. Some of the dishes they serve there are simply divine. We could go there someday...'

Sometime during the conversation, Abhigyan had emerged from his seat, circled around the table, and was now standing within an arm's distance of Ameena. Had he been sober enough to read the sensations on the girl's face, he would have read dread and horror writ large.

'Has anyone ever told you how pretty you are?' he continued, taking the liberty of using his forefinger to push a loosely dangling strand of hair behind her ear. She recoiled at his touch and retreating a couple of steps, she said, 'You are a big man saheb, and I am merely a worker here. You shouldn't be talking about such things with me.'

'What rubbish! Just because you don't come from money doesn't mean that you should be deprived of all the good things that life has to offer,' Abhigyan was saying even as he stepped closer to Ameena. She retreated further until her legs caught the hem of the waiting couch, unbalancing her momentarily. However, she held her ground, placing a hand on the wall behind her for support. 'Tell me what do you want and I will get it for you...earrings, a gold chain, what?' Abhigyan was barely a few inches away from her now. His eyes were dangerously amber and his transformed avatar was enough to send a chill up the sturdiest of spines. He looked no less than a monster at that moment.

He lifted his hands and rested them on her cheeks. She tried to push him back, and in that instant their interaction shattered all frontiers of civility and turned into a full-blown struggle. The petite Ameena proved no match for the sturdy doctor and she was soon pinned down on the couch, all her struggle notwithstanding. With his left hand Abhigyan held both her hands above her head while his right hand pushed her kurta towards her neck, baring her heaving torso. As soon as he had enough naked flesh in sight, he moved his right hand upwards and cupped her mouth with it. Even her screams were muffled now, as, like a cannibal, Abhigyan attacked her with his open mouth – biting and licking her breasts like a deranged man.

The monstrosity continued for several excruciating minutes, tiring both the tormentor and the tormented. Ameena's struggle was no longer as forceful now, and this Abhigyan construed as a sign of her surrender. Meaning to seize the opportunity to the fullest, he pulled his hands back and relegated them to unfastening his belt buckle. This was all the opening that Ameena needed. She folded both her legs up to her stomach and thrust them forward to land on Abhigyan's knees.

He let out a shriek, staggered back and clapped the floor with his back. Ameena didn't waste a single precious moment in looking at him or even straightening her clothes. She rushed out of the chamber and the clinic, running like a woman possessed. She remained running even when she had reached the main road, too scared to turn back, as though being chased by a pack of ravenous wolves.

It was when she very nearly collided with a speeding car that she finally stopped. The car had come to a screeching halt too and the driver had emerged from the vehicle hurling abuses at her. That was till he had set sight on her. One look at her and his anger evaporated in a flash. It was this kind man who dropped her to the nearest police station.

Her sobbing narrative of the incident was all it took, and a police van with four uniformed men and Ameena in tow was soon racing towards Dr. Abhigyan Kukreti's clinic.

The doctor was found sprawled on the couch in his chamber, his dishevelled clothes and half-unfastened belt recounting the horrific story that had played out a short while back. Dr. Kukreti did not offer any resistance, verbal or otherwise, as the policemen handcuffed him and dragged him out of his clinic. He didn't even spare the dishevelled Ameena a glance.

The newsmongers keeping a hawk's eye on the city's police stations had got their headline for the next morning – 'Doctor in the dock: prominent city doctor arrested on charges of sexual assault'.

30th December

It had been a long night and Junaid had hardly managed an eye-shut. The pain, like the violent eruptions of a flame on the verge of being extinguished, had returned with a tenacious fervour, leaving his Ammi twisting and turning on the bed all night. He had known of its return even as she had tried to swallow it, releasing her anguish ever so slowly in measured moans. He had remained passive though, opting to remain on his bed, allowing her to wage her battle unhindered. This was partly because there wasn't much he could do about her situation then, and more so since he knew that there was just the one dark night of suffering left for her to endure. The next morning she would get operated, and, God willing, the pain would only persist as a dreadful memory thereafter.

But in little time the casing of endurance had been breached and her moans had turned into full-blown screams. Ignorance was no longer an option. Junaid knew that if his Ammi was unable to contain the sting, it had well surpassed all defined levels of human tolerance. After all, who better to corroborate her strength and inner-will than the son who had been at their trying end for the better part of his life?

He got up, poured a glass of water from the earthen pot, shuffled through the rack where her medicines were kept and emerged on her bedside with the painkiller the doctor had prescribed for precisely such occurrences.

'It is worse than ever...,' his mother muttered, locking her misery-stricken eyes with his, as he used his free hand to prop her up. 'Allah... have mercy...,' she winced, struggling even to swallow the tiny pill.

The only thing worse than watching a loved one suffering is the realization of one's inability to alleviate their pain. To Junaid his mother's cries were nothing but a frustrating reminder of this feebleness – a mockery of his very existence. He could feel the sting of her pain in his own heart, like a dagger being plunged deeper with every scream she mouthed. His tear ducts were full, eager to let out a stream so as to drench his tumultuously pulsating emotions, but Junaid somehow managed to contain them. This was neither the time, nor the place to exhibit his own frailty. If anything, he needed to present a picture of confidence and strength for his mother's sake.

He remained seated by her bedside for whatever remained of the night, stroking her forehead, massaging her scalp and responding half-mindedly to her agony-induced ramblings. Soon the darkness began to scatter, overpowered by the bright of a new dawn. It was to be a cold morning, the chill in Junaid's unrested bones told him, but a significant one nevertheless. He had done all within his powers to make this day a reality and the only remaining piece was to ensure that his Ammi was comfortably delivered into the doctor's hands.

Last evening itself he had booked a taxi to ferry them to the clinic. It was a luxury he could afford, at least for now.

He was busy stuffing items he thought his Ammi might need during the day into a cloth bag when a knock sounded on the door. Junaid wearily glanced at his Ammi – exhaustion had finally got the better of her and she had fallen asleep. He was glad that the knock hadn't disturbed her. Next, he looked at the digital wristwatch strapped to his wrist, a rudimentary model that screamed 'Cheap' and 'China' but for its non-Mandarin numeric display. The taxi was expected to arrive only by the following hour, and he wasn't exactly expecting any visitors. With a frown-creased forehead he made for the door to answer the knock.

'She's asleep?' Jaya Chachi whispered through the partly open door. Junaid moved aside, allowing her room to step in, and nodded.

'It's fine, don't disturb her. I just got this for you,' she said, extending the cloth bag in her hand towards Junaid. Right behind her, Ajay too had stepped into the shanty by then. 'This is some food for both of you. She shouldn't be eating outside stuff at a time like this, you know.'

Junaid could say nothing but gratefully accept the parcel.

'I would have accompanied you to the hospital, but I can't afford to be absent from work today. I need to be there to keep an eye on the developments, you understand?' Ajay said, stepping closer to place his hands on Junaid's shoulders. His words had a mild overtone of conspiracy and Junaid understood the need for him to be at work perfectly well. Locking his gaze with Ajay's, he nodded his acquiescence.

'You will be back by the evening, right?'

'Inshallah…we should be,' Junaid responded.

When the mother-son duo departed, Junaid was left feeling heavy on the inside. It felt as if someone was squeezing him from within, making his bodily-fluids press hard against his casing with the intention of seeping out. His eyes were moist, blurring his immediate surroundings to him.

He let out a sigh and pulled the end of his t-shirt to wipe his eyes. It was an emotional moment alright, to find care and concern at the lowest ebbs of life, but he had more pressing issues at hand which needed his immediate attention. Jerking himself away from his thoughts, he got back to preparing for the long day that remained ahead.

The taxi arrived at the appointed hour. His Ammi wasn't screaming in pain now, but her condition seemed to have deteriorated drastically during the night. She looked frailer and weaker than ever. The few broken sentences she had uttered since waking up had appeared to be drawing energy from some inner reservoir within her – like an avaricious air conditioner sucking wattage from the meagre electric supply. It was only by leaning heavily on Junaid for support that she had been able to amble across to the waiting vehicle and board it.

It was excruciating to see the woman who had always stood by him like a sturdy pillar in such dire straits, but Junaid kept telling himself that the suffering was only momentary. She would soon be liberated from its deathly clutches and get back to being the strong and indefatigable woman he had known her to be.

The streets of Delhi were surprisingly empty for a Monday morning. Perhaps the city had decided to give itself a breather towards the fag end of another passing year. To Junaid this meant nothing. Alternating between his own thoughts and the need to keep a watch over his Ammi's condition, he didn't even realize when the taxi pulled up outside Dr. Abhigyan Kukreti's clinic.

Settling the fare, Junaid got down from the taxi. Swinging the bag with his mother's belongings over one shoulder, he helped her out, and clutching her frail frame with both hands, made for the clinic's entrance. He had visited the doctor only a few days back, but today the clinic appeared different. Despite the few people he could see idling about the entrance, there was a creepy, ominous discreetness to the place that he couldn't quite fathom.

A few more steps and he could see the reason behind this eerie feeling. The metallic grills outside the wooden door of the clinic were pulled together and a padlock holding them in their place announced that the place was shut. Junaid was perplexed. He glanced at his wristwatch – fifteen minutes to nine! He was due to see the doctor in fifteen minutes. How could the clinic be closed then?

He looked around, searching for a face that he could direct his questions to, but he had to quickly avert his gaze. The men he had noticed earlier, four in all, two of them seated on the wide steps leading to the clinic's entrance and one leaning against the outside wall, were all brazenly staring at him. They were eyeing him as though he were a sheep who had accidently wandered into the lion's den. Unease would be a mild word to describe what Junaid felt. The men didn't even look like distraught patients waiting for the clinic to open.

Even as he was assessing the surroundings, one man from among those seated on the steps, got up and stepped towards Junaid. He was officious looking, and a square black bag, like the ones used to store professional cameras and lenses, dangled in his hand.

'Yes?' he enquired.

'We are here to see the doctor,' Junaid, unsettled and surprised, managed to mutter.

'Oh, so you are his patient?' he enquired, scrutinizing the two even more closely with his penetrative gaze. 'Did you know him well?' he tentatively added even before Junaid could begin to answer.

'I had met him last week and he had called us here today. My mother needs to be operated upon. Why, what's the matter?'

'Well, the operation will have to wait,' the man responded with a smirk. 'The doctor, it seems, had other clandestine interests beyond simply treating his patients.'

'Meaning?'

The man briefly glanced at Junaid's Ammi and when convinced that she wasn't paying any particular attention to the conversation, said, 'He was arrested yesterday night for trying to rape one of his staff members.'

The revelation came as a blow for Junaid. He felt that the world around him had suddenly begun to spin manically. He couldn't think of anything to say and remained staring blankly at the man for several seconds.

'How do you know? And who are you?' he eventually managed to speak.

'The story is in the papers today; the whole world knows about it. We are from the press, waiting for his other employees to show up. Who knows what other concealed skeletons they might help us uncover. I don't think the doctor is going to be able to see any patients for some time now, so I suggest that you go take your mother to another doctor. She seems to be really unwell.'

'But I have already paid him his entire fees for the operation. Where will I get more money from now, and which doctor will be willing to carry out the operation at such short notice?' His ramblings, Junaid knew, were fruitless. The man he was speaking to was hardly in any position to help him. But he couldn't stop voicing his concerns. He had no idea what he was going to do next, and any guidance, no matter where it came from, was more than welcome.

'I understand, my friend, but there is nothing that can be done... Maybe you could wait with us for a while and see if any

driver who was not out to fleece him, and he led him to where he had left his Ammi waiting.

As he stepped out and approached her, he saw that her eyes were shut once again. She had probably fallen asleep while waiting for him.

'Ammi, here, have some water and then let's go. The taxi is waiting,' he said, extending the bottle of water in her direction. She didn't budge. Not a single batting of the lid, not a single twitch of a muscle.

Overcome by a sudden burst of panic, he dropped on his knees, and allowing the bottle in his hand to slip, reached out for her hands. Even before he could make an attempt to trace her pulse, by the sheer coldness of her touch, he knew that his Ammi was no more. Clutching her hands he slumped down, his senses too stunned to react and his eyes wide open in shock.

The fact that he was left alone in this world now took its time in sinking, rattling one part of him at a time. The first to come to terms with the loss were his eyes, letting out involuntary streams of tears from their sockets. Junaid was not crying though. He was like a statue in the middle of a fountain whose eyes the clever craftsman had chosen to be the outlets for oozing water. His mind was elsewhere, in a world of its own thoughts.

'Allah always keeps watch over his subjects… The kind of life we lead, the sort of deeds we do, that is what he uses to reward or chastise us in this life and thereafter,' his Ammi would often say. And he, for as far back as he remembered, had led a life teeming with immorality and corruption – stealing from others, cheating and deceiving them. Hell, even the money for his mother's treatment had been obtained from such unscrupulous means. So, was it possible that his Ammi's sufferings were but a manifestation of his own sins? Had her time truly come, or had he, her errant son, dragged her to an untimely death?

A section of his mind would attempt to come to his rescue: But what was I to do? I couldn't watch her suffer. I had to figure out a way to pay for her treatment, and had I tried doing so through legitimate means she wouldn't have lived to see that day anyway. She was my mother. And as a son wasn't it my duty to provide her the medical attention she needed, no matter what the cost?

However, the feeling of guilt was overpowering. Indeed, it was his duty as a son to provide for his mother, but not in a dishonest and disgraceful manner. What had his deceitful ways done for him in the end? Despite having acquired the money, could he provide her with the treatment he had hoped for? No!

Perhaps the doctor's arrest at the eleventh hour was God's way of making him pay for what he had done. Who knew what difficulties he had summoned upon the girl he had stolen the money from? What if she had lost her job? Maybe she too had an ailing parent at home that she needed to provide for.

Alright, he might not have been able to save her by simply mending his ways, but there was a chance that he could have prevented God's wrath from befalling her. In her lifetime she had done little to deserve a death as wretched and tragic as hers had been. To the least, she would have breathed her last in the confines of her home. She wouldn't then have found herself alone in her penultimate moments on the staircase of a strange building.

The hope of her revival had been so strong within Junaid that it had prevented any untoward thought from even surfacing. Resultantly, he had failed to bid her a final goodbye, to tell her how much he loved her and how meaningless his life would be without her. And this, to Junaid, was the telling blow that his karma had dealt him. He was shattered beyond resurrection and a part of him was still praying that this was all a horrible nightmare that he would soon wake up from.

He remained seated beside his dead mother, staring at her with blank but watery eyes for several hours, completely lost to the world around him. It was only towards the early evening, when a few passersby happened to notice the scene and approached him that Junaid eventually emerged from his trance. But his grief he would find hard to emerge from. It was going to stay with him, like an incessantly pricking thorn, for several months, years, or possibly even his entire lifetime.

Thereafter

The New Year had dawned with a feeling of discernible promise
for Sargam. It had been just a feeling, unsubstantiated and
vague, up until the previous evening.

The feeling perhaps stemmed from the fact that her
predicaments from the preceding week were a thing of the past
now. She had recovered the money that had been stolen from her,
at least most of it. The balance she had been able to reinstate from
her own savings, enabling its timely delivery to Ramamurthy as
she had pledged.

Mr. Ahuja had expressed some displeasure at the complications
she had managed to infuse into an otherwise simple task, but in
the end his loss had been covered and that is what mattered. Upon
hearing the entire account he had even feigned anger at the fact
that she hadn't shared the details with him in time, else he would
have done what he could to help her.

Sargam had a mind to remind him of his threat to have not only
her but her entire family 'rotting behind bars' when she had first
broken the news of the theft to him. But she somehow managed

to refrain from speaking her thoughts aloud. She realized that it was a mere rhetoric on part of her boss to assuage the ills that had passed between them, now that the issue had been favourably resolved. She noticed that despite his paternalistic stance, Mr. Ahuja had not made any offer to make good the unrecovered portion of the money that she had ended up contributing herself, but Sargam was beyond caring by then.

Another unexpected reprieve had come her way in the form of the news of Dr. Kukreti's arrest. The man was no saint and who better to vouch for that than Sargam. But the story, as she had come to know of it, had come as somewhat of a jolt even to her. Why would a man of his social standing engage in something so senseless and brash which could take away all that he had ever worked towards – his name, fame and fortune? Had his libidinal rush been so dominant and superseding that it had shrouded even his basic ability to think straight?

Moreover, the incident was timed to the same evening that she had planned to meet him. It was frightening for her to even imagine the sequence of events had it been her and not the hapless hired-help in Dr. Kukreti's proximity that evening. She was unable to shake the feeling that her failure to turn up for the meeting or accept his frenzied calls was at the core of the despicable occurrence. She felt terrible for the victim who had happened to be at the wrong place at the wrong time, but there was also the relief of knowing that the name in the newspaper reports could very well have been her own.

In the rush to withdraw money from the ATM and arrive in time for her meeting with Ramamurthy, she had failed to scan the newspapers that morning. It was Geeta who had called her, more a consolatory call than one meant to impart information. Her friend had been baffled by the fact that Sargam was clueless about such a telling development in the life of the man her family had been coaxing her to marry. Sargam had got a broad outline of the news story from Geeta, and later, while waiting for Ramamurthy in the hotel lobby, she had picked up a newspaper copy and gone through the gory details of it.

Surprisingly enough for her, the incident had never been raked up at home. Given Lalkrishna's penchant for newsprint and the fact that the media had latched on to the story like a fly does to a mound of jaggery, it was highly unlikely that he was unaware of the developments. He had however refrained from raising the subject in Sargam's presence, a meek surrender in light of the changed circumstances perhaps. As for Sargam, she was only too happy to let go of the opportunity to blow her victory trumpet. She knew that Dr. Abhigyan Kukreti, and as a consequence the topic of her marriage, would not be raised within the household in the near future and this was good enough a consolation as far as she was concerned.

The only real trouble that had breached the change of the calendar year for her was the loss of her regular means of transport. With Sharib gone, she was once again left to the mercy of the Delhi auto-wallahs to be ferried to office and back. But that too was a problem she could afford to brush under the carpet for the next fortnight at least.

The last evening, just before dinner she had received a call from her brother Lalit on her mobile phone.

'I am coming to India for good,' Lalit had said after the exchange of their usual banter. 'Don't tell Mummy-Papa as yet; I want this to be a surprise for them.'

'When? How come?' she had nearly screamed. The excitement was too much for her to contain, but she was cognizant of the fact that her excited voice might lead to undue curiosity among her parents. So, keeping a deliberate check on her volume she inundated him with a barrage of questions.

During the course of the conversation she learnt that Lalit had made good money during the course of a few odd jobs (he didn't care to elaborate what) and was now desirous of returning to his motherland. He intended to open a restaurant in Delhi and had even hinted that he would be happy if Sargam chose to join his enterprise. But that was a matter for future deliberation. What remained of immediate significance was that he was landing in Delhi the very next evening.

It was with much difficulty that she had managed to check her enthusiasm from exposing itself to her parents over dinner. And late into the night she had remained thinking about all that Lalit and she needed to catch up on and reminiscing the happy times she had shared with her brother in a past that no longer seemed distant.

Upon reaching office, the first thing she had done was to walk into Mr. Ahuja's cabin and request for a two week leave. There had been some resistance as he recounted the list of tasks that were likely to come up within that period, but her resolute persistence saw her through in the end. Albeit reluctantly, but Mr. Ahuja did find it in him to scribble his initials on her leave application. And now, as she was on her way to the airport to receive Lalit, the world around her appeared to be brimming with an unspoken promise.

◆

The rickety state-transport bus was curving down its ordained path, snarling and spurting on the half-concrete, half-dust national highway. The driver seemed in some sort of urgency as he sped past barren fields, desolate clusters of trees, mud-brick houses and bunches of inappropriately clothed kids. It was half past ten in the morning and there weren't too many vehicles on the road yet. This sleepy part of the country was still waking up to a new day.

Most windows of the bus, at least the ones with intact glass-panes and operative hinges, were shut to prevent the chilly breeze from inconveniencing passengers. And those that were forced to remain open had occupants of the adjacent seats recoiling as far away from the gushing wind as they could, all but one. This solitary window had a face staring blankly out into the horizon. It was a pretty, expressionless face bordered by a black dupatta. It was evident that either the cold winds had impaled her to a point where she could feel them no more, or she was deliberately trying to punish herself, testing her endurance in some warped way.

The girl was travelling unaccompanied; an unusual occurrence for the eastern parts of Uttar Pradesh, and this prevented the few concerned co-passengers who had been observing her for a while now from making an approach. However, Ameena Khatun could care no less. She had taken the overnight train to Lucknow from Delhi, and from there, the first bus out for Azamgarh. It had been a strenuous journey so far, but she couldn't feel the discomfort. This was nothing in comparison to the agony and suffering she had had to endure over the past few weeks of her life.

Ameena had been lured to Delhi by the unblemished desires of her heart. Sharib, the only man she had ever set a longing eye on in her lifetime was in Delhi and she had simply followed him there. Only, hers wasn't a story about the union of two aching hearts. Instead, it had turned out more like a never-ending quest.

She had known Sharib from the time they were both just kids – he, quiet and introvert, and she, his self-appointed guardian angel. There was something about the boy that had drawn her towards him from the word go. Of course there was the sympathy of watching him go about life without any real friends and the protective streak that comes ever so naturally to womankind, but in this case there always was that something extra. Ameena had been happy to take up the vacant slot of his only friend back then.

Eventually time and societal norms veered them apart, but not so further apart that it could prevent her from keeping a watch over him. She had keenly watched him grow into a level-headed, good-looking young man from a distance, making her presence felt only when it was appropriate to do so. She was still protective about him, and to her, this was but an extension of the friendship they had once shared.

It was when her Abba had mentioned the possibility of a marital alliance between Sharib and her that her mind along with her heart had started treading on uncharted frontiers. She had suddenly come alive to the possibility of spending her entire life with Sharib, and armed with this hopefulness she had begun to recount their happy moments together and all that she had observed of him, always with a content smile. In the privacy of her thoughts, she had started constructing a whole new world inhabited by just the two of them. She had even found a name for what she had always felt for Sharib, right from their childhood days – Love. Yes, she was in love with Sharib, she had always been; only she had been ill-equipped to identify her own emotions earlier.

But seldom do things shape the way we dream for them to, and this proved true even in Ameena's case. Just when she was hoping to be informed of the date for her impending Nikah with Sharib, she learnt that he was heading to Delhi to earn a living. She knew that behind his malleable exterior, Sharib was a ferociously ambitious man and she didn't want to stand as a hindrance in his path. Although she was mildly peeved at the timing of his decision, she decided against confronting him over it, whereby depriving herself of the only real opportunity to communicate with him directly on the matter.

Ameena, in a bid to assuage her frustrations, had been telling herself that it was only a matter of time and when Sharib would find his footing in the city, he would return to marry her. Her dreams had remained the same, of Sharib and their living happily together, she cooking for him and he pampering her at the slightest of pretexts. Only the setting had changed from their village in Azamgarh district to the city of Delhi.

But the wait was proving excruciating. Days turned into weeks and weeks into months and no news of Sharib came her way. She would visit his house regularly, chat-up with his Ammi, help with the household chores, posing as a thoughtful neighbour, but all with the ulterior motive of getting some news about Sharib. And then, a few months back, she learnt that Sharib would be visiting home. She made it a point to be present at his house when he came, hoping to see a glint of joy in his eyes at the surprise. None emerged.

She knew that his was a short visit and when she saw no initiative regarding their marriage from his side, she decided to confront him – their first direct communication on the matter. But Sharib remained evasive, avoiding any kind of commitments, infuriating Ameena to no mean degree. She felt hurt and cheated, but more than anything, she was furious with herself for allowing her destiny to chart its own course unobstructed. It was about time she reclaimed the reins to her life and reached out for what she desired. She gave Sharib a piece of her mind before walking out on him, but the plan to follow him to Delhi had already begun to form within her head by then.

The thought that perhaps Sharib did not reciprocate the love she felt for him did cross her mind, but she was too hurt, too pained to allow it to jeopardize her plans. If he didn't love her, she was going to ensure that he began to, and for that she needed to be in his proximity. It wasn't easy to convince her parents, but her resolve left little room for negotiations. The fact that she had relatives in Delhi, whom she could put up with, helped and in the end her family was compelled to yield to her wishes.

She managed to reach Delhi and even succeeded in reopening the avenues of communication with Sharib, but the thing she failed to factor into her plans were the demands that a big city made of its habitants. Her relatives had graciously provided her a roof, but the need to figure out a way to provide for her own self was still looming large. She was forced to take up a job with a utilities services company to make her ends meet, and before she could even realize, she had been swallowed by the rut of earning her daily bread. Her primary purpose behind coming to Delhi was still firmly enshrined within her, but it had inadvertently slipped a pedestal or two within her list of immediate priorities.

It was at this juncture that all hell broke loose. She found herself embroiled in an incident so horrific and appalling that it forced her to change her entire outlook towards humanity and life. Her employer, a doctor of prominence and otherwise a pleasant-seeming man, tried to force himself upon her. Her modesty outraged and her senses numbed, she managed to flee from the site like a hunted prey running for its life. The experience shattered her from within, razing to dust her pride and self-esteem, leaving a blotch on her that was not going to be erased anytime soon.

The one thing she craved for in these trying times was a loving shoulder to lean on, but none materialized. Sharib didn't even bother to pay her a visit. She was disillusioned and traumatized. And yet, when a few days had passed, she decided to visit him instead. It was perhaps the flame of love that refused to extinguish no matter how trying were the storms it faced.

Sharib wasn't home. Instead she met his roommate Afzal. Afzal was aware of the tragedy to have befallen her and seemed sincerely apologetic about it. But when it came to sharing Sharib's whereabouts, his explanations sounded as hollow as the inside of a drum. Sharib had gone out of station on work, he said, but when she probed further about the work or even his destination, he feigned ignorance. Was it even possible that Sharib had left home without even telling his roommate where he was going, for what, or when was he expected to return?

The answer was obvious, but Ameena chose to play along, searching for clues to help reinforce the only explanation for his absence that was coming into her mind. Sharib had decided to ignore her. He had chosen this delicate juncture to expel her from his life, perhaps because he felt that now, when she was at her frailest, the blow will prove the most telling.

She asked Afzal for a phone number she could reach him on; he had none. 'He said that where he was going, his Delhi number wouldn't work,' he added for good measure. If the word lame needed an example, this was it. She stomped out of the room and out of Sharib's life for the one last time. The blow was indeed devastating. It had smashed to bits not only her dreams, but any remnants of faith on humanity that the events of the preceding days had left within her.

Her decision was made. She had no option but to return to the world she had left behind in her quest to find true love. True love, if ever such a thing existed, was not hers to find.

And now, when she was only a few hours away from reuniting with her past, she was struggling to snap the mental ties that bound her to the world she was leaving behind. It was going to prove an uphill task, she knew, but once again she was up for the challenge.

◆

He sat propped against the wall, intently focused on his toenails, using his fingers to scratch some invisible layering off them. He had been doing this for nearly an hour now, pausing only to pull back his feet so as to fit his frame in the minimum possible space. Had he bothered to look up, the purple-black bruise enveloping his left eye, the disproportionately swollen corner of his lips and a generally dishevelled face would have come visible.

It hadn't been particularly long, but Sharib had already lost count of the number of days he had spent locked up in this enclosure. It wasn't quite like anything he had seen in the movies – dingy little rooms used for confining one or at the most two convicts at a time. Given a choice he would have readily opted to shift into one of those supposed cells. In the movies the prisoners at least had enough space to straighten their limbs. Here he did not enjoy that luxury.

For the first two nights post his arrest, he had been lodged in the lockup at the Srinivaspuri Police Station. No less than a superfluity in the hindsight. On the third day he was taken to court by a couple of policemen, and once his bail application had been summarily rejected by the sitting magistrate, he had been herded into a van with a horde of others and dropped off at his present abode – one of the many enclosures used for housing under trials within the Tihar Jail complex.

It was a large hall, about a thousand square feet in size, with a waist-high partition towards its rear concealing the washbasin and the latrine. There were no other fixtures – no fans, no lights and no furniture – between the partition on one end and the prison bars on the other. Originally it would have been designed to house 25 to 30 people at best, but on last count the hall where Sharib was seated was home to over 150 undertrials. At night the men were forced to sleep on their sides so as to accommodate as many on the floor as was possible. Some unfortunate ones were still left squatting, propped against the walls for the night. If someone wished to use the toilet at night, he simply could not, because of two reasons: first, it was impossible to take even a single step without stepping on someone else, and second, even the floor immediately circling the pot was carpeted with sleeping bodies.

Some of the injury marks Sharib bore were a gift from the policemen at Srinivaspuri, but most of them he had acquired after shifting to this facility. For the older inmates it was a sort of recreational engagement to maul the newbies. Sharib had quickly realized that there were two ways to survive this torture – he could either align himself with one or the other closely-knit gang that operated within the enclosure or he could lie low and wait for the new batch of inmates to arrive or hope that his tormentors quickly got bored with him. He opted for the second strategy. It succeeded as well, as he surreptitiously dropped from the eyes of his tyrants, but not before they had left him with enough to remember them by.

Sharib didn't know what the 'hell' from the afterlife looked like, but to him this was Jahannum – a hell for the living. In his few days here he had witnessed such acts of barbarianism that he was convinced that a worse place simply could not exist, not in this world and not in the one after. He had seen men being ruthlessly pulped, he had witnessed groups of men forcibly sodomising a weaker one in full view of others, and he had seen these vicious acts being wholeheartedly cheered by the onlookers. The physical pain and the mental agony of just being there was tremendous, but it was still dwarfed by the anguish that Sharib had been concealing within.

Why was he here at all? On charges of stealing! But he had not stolen a single penny from anyone. The only crime he had committed was the crime of love, and he was guilty on two counts – of having loved someone unconditionally and of having failed to reciprocate the love of someone who had loved him just as absolutely.

The day Sharib was arrested had unfolded into one of the gloomiest days of his life. He had grown up hearing that all good deeds are rewarded in this very life. But his had landed him on the wrong side of the law, making him the subject of the Delhi Police's infamous brutality. He was only trying to help the girl he loved in her hour of need and he was expecting no accolades for this, but what he got in return wasn't something he had bargained for either.

The moment of truth had occurred when he had been brought to face Sargam. The look of abhorrence, of utter detestation in her eyes, he would not forget till his last living breath. 'Yes, that's him,' she had said, reducing his existence to a beastly encumbrance in a fraction of a second. In a single sweep she had erased all the words that had ever been exchanged between them, those that Sharib's effervescent imagination had used as a base for his love-induced fantasies, and turned him into a complete stranger. Whether it was the hurt of having been wronged, or the insignificant abstraction he had been reduced to in her eyes, he couldn't tell, but this blow had been far more tearing than any physical ones he had ever endured.

Apart from Sargam, Afzal was the only other non-uniformed person to be aware of his arrest and Sharib had sworn him to complete secrecy even as the policemen were dragging him out of his residence, especially with regards to Ameena. He was aware of her feelings for him and knew that she would do all in her capacity to help secure his release. However, he thought it unfair to trouble her over an action of his, the very basis of which was his love for another woman.

Afzal had visited him in the lockup and in the courthouse the next morning, seeking Sharib's guidance on what he could do to help. Sharib hadn't been able to think of anything. Afzal had neither the resources, financial or otherwise, nor the acumen to turn things around. His intent, no matter how unblemished, wasn't going to prove of much use to Sharib. As for Afzal, while he had lived up to his promise of not sharing Sharib's whereabouts with Ameena, he had also withheld the information about her troubles from him. Sharib was in enough mess already and he saw no point in burdening him further with things he could do nothing about.

The court had rejected Sharib's bail plea, filed by a court-appointed lawyer on his behalf, and for the past several days he had been languishing in this particular enclosure of the Tihar Jail. If there was one thing Sharib had in abundance here, it was time. Time to think, to mull over what he had done and where he had gone wrong, and thinking he had been doing.

His anger with Sargam for judging him the way she had was no longer as intense. In fact, he had brought himself to empathize with her standpoint. All evidence had been stacked up against him and he had given her no reasons to believe otherwise. It was only natural for her to think that it was he who had stolen the money, was it not? And perhaps the fury he had seen in her eyes was a manifestation of the hurt she felt at having been cheated by someone she thought she could trust.

No sooner had he reached neutral grounds with respect to his feelings towards Sargam, the fantasies from his past once again began to consume him – If she had once trusted him, maybe there was a chance that she could do so again? Would she be waiting for him when he got out of prison? Once she got to learn the facts of the case, she was bound to feel guilty. She would probably offer a teary-eyed apology for all that he was forced to endure, and he would forgive her. This time he would not waste any time in telling her exactly what he felt with regards to her. How would she react to it? Would she blush? Would she smile? Or, would she reach out and hug him?

Sometimes his thoughts darted towards Ameena as well, just about as frequently as he thought about his family, about Afzal and about the quantum of work he would need to put in to resurrect his life once he got out. These were the more pragmatic among his musings. He couldn't help feeling bad for Ameena, for her love going unrequited. But he absolved himself of any guilt in this regard by arguing that he had never led her to believe that he loved her. He had never even consented to marry her, and if she couldn't come to terms with this reality, there was little he could do. It is just a matter of time, he would tell himself, and she will realize the futility of her efforts. He prayed that she returned to the village soon and settled down with a nice, loving husband. 'She is a nice girl and deserves much better from her life.'

And today too Sharib was lost in the world of his own thoughts. The scratching of nails was merely an involuntary action his body had come up with to keep itself occupied as he dived in and out of a pool of his emotions. Within his head he was conjuring scenes from a script he had prepared just the preceding night – of Sargam and him returning to his village in Azamgarh and living happily thereafter. Love, a strange emotion that makes people do the strangest of things, isn't it?

www.ingramcontent.com/pod-product-compliance
Lightning Source LLC
Chambersburg PA
CBHW060118260626
47160CB00005B/1923